"Please, Raphael— can't you just let it go?" gr 93

"I can't let it go because I don't know why you left me, Annis," Raphael muttered. "And until I do, I shan't be able to forget you. There's too much unfinished business between us. I keep wondering why, why..."

He looked down, his face hard, then suddenly caught her face between his hands.

"No," she groaned.

"Yes," he said thickly. "There's something I have to know!" and his lips closed over hers. Annis was lost from the moment their mouths met, her mind submerged between crashing waves of pleasure.

When at last Raphael lifted his head they were both breathing raggedly. "You couldn't kiss me like that, and be indifferent," Raphael said huskily.

CHARLOTTE LAMB began to write "because it was one job I could do without having to leave the children." Now writing is her profession. She has had more than forty Harlequin novels published since 1978. "I love to write," she explains, "and it comes very easily to me." She and her family live in a beautiful old home on the Isle of Man, between England and Ireland. Charlotte spends eight hours a day writing—and enjoys every minute of it.

Books by Charlotte Lamb

A VIOLATION
SECRETS

HARLEQUIN PRESENTS
1202—DESPERATION
1236—SEDUCTIVE STRANGER
1290—RUNAWAY WIFE
1345—RITES OF POSSESSION
1370—DARK PURSUIT
1393—SPELLBINDING

HARLEQUIN ROMANCE
2696—KINGFISHER MORNING
2804—THE HERON QUEST
2950—YOU CAN LOVE A STRANGER

Don't miss any of our special offers. Write to us at the following address for information on our newest releases.

Harlequin Reader Service
P.O. Box 1397, Buffalo, NY 14240
Canadian address: P.O. Box 603,
Fort Erie, Ont. L2A 5X3

CHARLOTTE LAMB

dark music

Harlequin Books

TORONTO • NEW YORK • LONDON
AMSTERDAM • PARIS • SYDNEY • HAMBURG
STOCKHOLM • ATHENS • TOKYO • MILAN

Harlequin Presents first edition November 1991
ISBN 0-373-11410-9

Original hardcover edition published in 1990
by Mills & Boon Limited

DARK MUSIC

CHAPTER ONE

ANNIS saw the poster for the concert as she was walking through the flea market in search of a present for her mother. She stopped in the middle of the narrow, winding street so suddenly that she almost got run over by an ancient taxi. The driver leaned out and yelled furiously in Greek. Annis tore her eyes away from the name printed in huge black letters on the poster, and muttered, 'Sorry!'

The taxi driver's face changed. 'Ah! English!' he said to himself in a meaningful tone, as if that explained everything. His black eyes surveyed her from head to toe, and he nodded. Even if she hadn't spoken he would probably have guessed her nationality anyway. Her pale blue linen suit had that classic English cut and style and Annis had classic looks: cool blue English eyes, a slender figure, long, graceful legs, smooth pale blonde hair worn in a chignon, delicate, pale skin which did not like the sun and looked almost transparent, like fine English bone china. The driver grinned, showing a gold tooth. 'English lady, you want taxi?'

Annis abandoned any idea of shopping; she was in no mood now to do anything but get back to her hotel to think. She nodded and climbed into the vehicle which rattled away at reckless speed back up the hill towards Syntagma Square and her hotel, the Grand Bretagna. The driver talked almost as fast as his taxi moved; his English was good and he was friendly, but Annis couldn't keep her mind on what he said. She smiled whenever he looked at her, and nodded, but she was stunned by disbelief and anxiety and couldn't think of anything else.

There was nothing to worry about! she reassured herself. The concert was tomorrow night and her coach party left Athens at seven o'clock in the morning. In all probability, the orchestra was still on its way here—she knew how tightly these tour schedules were meshed, and they might not even arrive until she was out of Athens, and even if they had got here they would probably be staying at some other hotel. There was no chance of running into anyone, none whatever.

Yet she was sweating, her clothes sticking to her, as she headed into the hotel. She needed a shower, and then she would lie down.

Her head had begun to bang like a bass drum and she had trouble summoning a smile for the porter as she collected her key from his desk. She and Loveday were sharing the large twin room, but it would be empty at the moment. Loveday wouldn't be back for hours; she and Carl had gone to visit an old friend of their family, a retired businessman, who lived by the sea a few miles outside Athens, at Vouliagmeni.

'Come with us,' Carl had said. 'Petros won't mind. He's very hospitable. We're going to have a poolside barbecue—doesn't that sound great?'

Annis hadn't known what to say; she wouldn't have felt at ease visiting a total stranger who had not invited her, but that would never occur to either Carl or his sister. Nothing bothered them or threw them off balance. They were from a wealthy background, and had grown up very sure of themselves. Annis envied them, but she couldn't imitate them, so she had given Carl an apologetic smile, shaking her head. 'Thanks, but I promised myself one last walk around Athens before we leave. I saw some very pretty jewellery on a market stall that would be a perfect present for my mother.'

'I don't think you should walk so far in this heat,' Loveday had said, frowning. Loveday was a redhead and had to wear a hat or she was likely to get sunstroke, so she took great care not to be out in the sun for long. Annis had smiled at her reassuringly.

'I'll wear a hat, don't worry!'

'Mind you do!' Carl had stressed. He and Loveday were twins, not identical, but still very alike in every way, their hair was the same fiery shade, their eyes a warm, sunny greeny-brown, and they were both prone to burning in the sun.

'I'll just stroll along and keep in the shade as much as I can,' Annis had promised them. 'I'll be fine. You two go and enjoy yourselves and I'll see you at breakfast tomorrow morning.'

'Breakfast?' Carl had grimaced. 'Coffee and a roll, that's all we'll get, and then we have the drive through the mountains to Corinth ahead of us, on an almost empty stomach.'

'All you think about is food!' Loveday had teased. 'And this coach trip was your idea!'

Carl had grinned at her. 'And a brilliant idea, too, wasn't it, Annis? If I hadn't talked you both into coming on this tour you would be lying on a beach in Spain right now, bored out of your skull and sizzling in the sun like sausages.'

'Sounds wonderful,' Loveday had sighed. 'Talking of beaches, shall we get going? I want to get my bikini wet. What this hotel needs is a swimming-pool—don't you agree, Annis?'

Annis had agreed, she would have liked a swim herself, but it would be nice to have a few hours alone, too. She liked being with Loveday and Carl, but time to yourself was an essential on a trip like this one, although the other two never seemed to think so. They were gregarious souls, perhaps because they were twins and had grown up accustomed to having company all the time.

She had waved them off from the hotel steps before setting out herself. At the time she had been relieved to be alone, but now she wished she had gone with them; if she had, she wouldn't have seen that poster, or known who was going to be in Athens tomorrow night.

She pressed the button for the fifth floor; the lift shot upwards, and Annis tried to think about something else, anything else—oh, it was so stupid to get worked up over a mere coincidence! What did it matter, after all, if there was to be a concert in Athens tomorrow night? The orchestra performed in London often enough without her getting into a state of witless confusion.

The doors opened and she stepped out, almost colliding with a man waiting to enter the lift.

'Sorry!' they both automatically murmured, and then their eyes met. Annis turned white, lips parting on an audible, shocked intake of air. The man had lost colour, too, his skin tightening over his facial bones.

'You!' he muttered, and the sound of his voice sent her into desperate panic. She ducked under his arm and ran.

Her room was close to the lifts; she had the key in her hand, but she was trembling so violently that she couldn't get it into the lock at first, and by the time she did and managed to open the door he had caught up with her.

'Oh, no, you don't!' he grated. 'You aren't running away this time!'

He pushed her into the room, and she backed, her throat so tight that she couldn't have got a sound out if she had tried. He slammed the door shut with his foot and stood there, staring at her fixedly, as if half inclined to doubt his own eyes. She knew how he probably felt; she was incredulous herself. It was against all the laws of probability for them to meet here, in the same hotel, so far away from London.

She didn't look at him—she looked at the floor—but she saw him, all the same, his image imprinted on her retina under her lowered lids: a dark, hostile face, finely sculpted, the face of a man of great power and sensitivity, his nose well shaped, his mouth strong, rather grimly set at this moment, his eyes piercing, an icy grey.

He had changed, she thought with a shock, although it was two years since she had last seen him, and what did she expect? Everybody changed as time went by; she knew he must see differences in her. She was not merely two years older, she had known great pain and loneliness during those years. He had changed more radically, though, surely? He had always been slim and fit, but he had lost weight visibly, grown fleshless, physically tougher, his body as tense as a drawn bowstring and his features bleakly austere.

Annis shivered, thinking, He's a stranger. I don't know this man, but then, did I ever know him?

'What are you doing in Athens?' he bit out, and she jumped.

'I . . . I'm on holiday.'

'Holiday?' he repeated in a blank voice, as though she had surprised him. Yet what answer had he expected?

'A coach tour of Greece.' Annis moistened her dry lips with her tongue. Hadn't she read somewhere that talking defused a tense situation? She went on hurriedly, voice husky, 'We flew into Athens three days ago, and we've been on coach trips to Sounion and Piraeus, and visited the museums and galleries—all the usual touristy things, I suppose.' She tried a rather unsteady laugh.

'My favourite was the Parthenon—it was almost invisible in smog the first day, but when we went up there it was magical, and I liked the Plaka and the flea market, too.'

He just stood there, staring at her, and nervously she went on, 'And...and tomorrow we're moving on to Corinth for two days.'

'We?'

The word exploded in the quiet room and she looked up in shock, her dark blue eyes very wide, the pupils dilated, glossy black.

'Who are you with?' he curtly asked.

'I told you...a coach party...' She couldn't hold his stare, though; she looked away and saw herself in the mirror on the dressing-table, her face very white and her eyes looking like purple anemones, the Greek windflowers, with their smudged, sooty centres, or was that just because she was trembling so much? Anemones trembled; was that why they were called windflowers? I feel as if I'm feverish, she thought. I'm thinking in a crazy way; I must try to pull myself together. But having him there, so close to her, in the same room, made it impossible for her to think clearly. The hostility, the contempt in his face was intolerable. She deserved it, she couldn't deny that, but that did not make it any easier to bear.

'You can't have come on holiday alone,' he brusquely dismissed. 'So who did you come with? The one you left me for?'

His voice was a slap in the face, and he took a step as he spoke. Her nerves leapt and she moved too, hastily, several steps back, watching him like a cornered animal watching the hunter which has trapped it.

His mouth twisted cynically. 'Oh, don't worry, no need to look like that. I wouldn't lay a hand on you. There was a time when I felt like killing you, but that was a long time ago and I'm over it now. I don't give a damn whether you're still with the guy you walked out with, or you've chucked him over too and moved on to someone else. I only asked out of casual curiosity.'

Annis hated the barbed contempt in his voice; her blue eyes flashed with an answering rage. 'Don't talk to me like that!'

'What's the matter, Annis—does the truth sting?' he mocked harshly.

'It isn't the truth! I'm not like that!' she whispered, but she knew she was wasting her breath. Whatever she said, he would go on despising her, and she couldn't blame him. In his place, she would feel the same.

'Aren't you?' His eyes moved from her to flick around the twin-bedded room. Annis watched him register the fact that both beds were turned down, ready for occupation. His brows drew tighter and his mouth hardened. 'And I suppose he isn't sharing this room with you, either?'

'I'm sharing it with a girl from the office!' Annis ran across the room and threw open the wardrobe doors, pointing to the clothes inside. 'See? Both sides...just women's clothes. Look in the chest of drawers, too. And if you look under the pillows on the beds, you'll just find nightdresses.'

He shrugged. 'I'll take your word for it. So, why isn't he with you? Quarrelled with him?'

He wasn't going to let the subject go, she realised, a sigh shaking her. 'Please...' she muttered. 'I'm sorry about what happened...There's no way I can explain, but I am sorry, and please...go away...leave me alone...'

She stood there, her neck curved in an attitude of defeat, her head lowered, her hands hanging at her sides, and for a long moment he stood still on the other side of the room, watching her. She could hear the rough drag of his breathing, she felt the rage and tension in him, and her body shook with pain and fear of what might be coming.

'Just a letter,' he said thickly. 'You couldn't even face me, you just wrote a letter saying it was all over, and then you vanished. Didn't I deserve to be told to my face what was wrong, why you had changed your mind? For God's sake, why couldn't you see me and talk about it?'

Annis was afraid to move, or look at him. Her voice was a faint thread of sound he had to concentrate on to hear. 'I couldn't see you face to face. Look at you now, you're frightening when you're angry!' The dark side of his nature came out in his music too; you heard it clearly then, revealed in raw sound, where words could not conceal the male force, the aggression buried deep in his psyche.

'Frightening!' he exploded and she tightened further, trying to stop herself shaking. 'Are you trying to blame me now? Isn't that typical of a woman? Whatever she does it's always the man's fault! It could never be you to blame, could it? Oh, no, you're perfect, you're just a victim, a wronged innocent!'

'I didn't say that!' she muttered feverishly. 'It was just one of those things. I'm not accusing you, of course I'm not. You're angry with me, and I'm sorry, but it's two years ago, it's over, can't we forget it?'

'Forget it?' he snarled, even angrier at that for some reason, his face darkly flushed. 'No, Annis, I can't damned well forget it!' You dumped me without explaining why and ever since you've been under my skin, like one of those burrowing insects, a constant irritation, driving me crazy, wondering why...why...' He came towards her, his eyes glittering. 'I want to know...why...'

There was a tap on the door and they both froze, listening.

'Your friend back?' he muttered.

Before she could answer, a voice said something in Greek and then there was the sound of a key in the lock and the door opened. A chamber-maid stood there, a pile of clean towels over her arm. Startled to see them, she muttered an apology, about to back out again, and Annis hurriedly said, 'No, please, you want to change the towels? Of course, come in...'

She felt the quick, deadly look he gave her, but pretended not to be aware of it. The girl nodded and walked across to the bathroom. Annis quietly said to the silent man, 'Please go. I'm sorry, but there's nothing else to say. I have to get to sleep early, we're leaving at first light.'

For a moment she was afraid he would refuse to leave. Her nerves flickered wildly as his hands clenched, his mouth drew tight, but after giving her one last, long stare, as if imprinting her on his memory—or expunging her forever, perhaps—he walked past her to the door and was gone.

Annis stood there, shaking from head to foot in helpless reaction to the last half-hour. She was in shock. She had seen him again; he had been here, she had seen him, heard his voice—and now he had gone. She couldn't believe it.

The chamber-maid came out of the bathroom, smiled at her curiously, and went out, saying in thickly accented English, 'Goodnight, miss.'

Annis automatically answered, smiled, but was hardly aware of her at all.

Over the past two years she had often daydreamed about seeing him again, what they might say, how he might look at her, but she hadn't imagined anything like this bitter reality. She had not wanted to imagine it like that, of course. She had been dreaming of a very different scenario, but in her secret heart she had always known that if they did ever meet again he would be bitterly hostile. He hated her. She had known he would, and there was nothing she could do about it.

She wished she could reverse the flow of time and get back to where they had been before that last night, but time did not flow backwards any more than rivers flowed uphill. You couldn't turn back the clock, you could only face things as they were and go on with your life, and that was what she had done over the past two years. What had happened had been like some appalling accident that left you alive, but maimed. To survive, you had to find a way of coping with what had happened to you, and before you could do that you had to come to terms with yourself. She had done, somehow; she had rebuilt her shattered life, and slowly begun to feel happy and confident again, but tonight she found that carefully reconstructed world in pieces around her once more.

When Loveday crept into their room around midnight, Annis lay very still and pretended to be asleep, but she wished even more now that she had gone to Vouliagmeni to the poolside barbecue. Her holiday in Greece would not have been ruined, she would not be taking around with her everywhere she went the memory of those contemptuous, distaste-filled grey eyes.

In the morning Loveday gave her a puzzled, anxious look. 'Hey! You look terrible! You aren't ill, are you?'

Annis lied. 'I must have eaten something that disagreed with me.'

'I've got some pills for it, although in Greece the food is so good I didn't think we would need to worry about digestive problems!' Loveday carried a whole pharmacy around with her, and soon dug out some pills which

Annis accepted, but only pretended to take. 'You'd better not eat any breakfast until you've got over it,' said Loveday, and Annis agreed. She wasn't hungry, anyway, and now she would not need to explain why she wasn't able to face her light breakfast of rolls, coffee and fruit juice. It was harder to bear Carl's and Loveday's affectionate concern, though, knowing that she had lied to them. Annis hated to tell them lies.

A sigh escaped her. Hadn't she been lying to them about certain things ever since she'd met them? Naturally, they had asked her questions about herself, and there were some things she had not told them. She hadn't actually lied, she thought defensively—she simply had not told them everything. But she had allowed them to make mistaken assumptions about her, and that was lying, in a way.

They had known her such a short time, although the three of them had come to know each other very well. Or felt they did, she admitted guiltily. Carl and Loveday thought she was an open book to them. Her life didn't sound terribly action-crammed, the way she had told it. She had lived with her mother in Manchester until they moved down to London so that her mother could look after her frail older brother who was rarely able to leave his bed. He did not need nursing—he was not actually ill most of the time, simply very weak with an incurable but slow-acting disease—but he did need company and loving care, both of which he got from Mrs Hilton, who was happy to have someone to look after again. She had always been very fond of her only brother, and when illness had struck him down she had immediately made up her mind to sell her house and move in with him.

The move down south had come at an opportune time for Annis. She had not been intending to move with her mother, at first; she had thought she would be staying in Manchester, but her life had suddenly been blown apart and she had needed desperately to get away. Her mother had gently suggested that she should come to London too, and Annis had gratefully accepted. There was plenty of room in her uncle's house, which was a large Victorian one in Croydon.

She was a good secretary; she had had no difficulty getting another job, in the centre of London with an advertising agency, and it was there that she had met Loveday, who worked in the art department doing graphics. Carl was a copywriter in the firm, which had been founded by their uncle. Annis had got on with them very well from the start, although their background was very different from her own. Her family had never had much money, but Carl and Loveday came from a wealthy family, and they always carried the high gloss of moneyed assurance.

They boarded their coach at seven o'clock outside the hotel. Athens was already choked with traffic; horns blaring, cars edged along Syntagma Square in the sunlight, which filtered down through palm leaves in the National Gardens on the other side of the square and glittered on the windows of the Parliament building. Annis queued up with the other passengers to climb into the coach, which was still being loaded with their luggage. She was not the only one to have a pale face and weary eyes. One American woman yawned, then apologised to her with a rueful smile.

'I got to bed late last night. We thought we'd have a final fling around Athens, seeing the nightlife. Boy, was that a mistake! We had a great time, but I only got four hours' sleep, and now I feel like death. These early starts are killers, aren't they?'

'Well, we shall be in Corinth for a couple of days, so you can catch up on your sleep there!' soothed Paddy, their courier, overhearing this.

'As soon as we hit the next hotel I'm going to bed and staying there for a long time, believe me!' the American woman said.

Loveday was looking up at the classical white façade of the hotel. 'I wonder how old it is.'

'Victorian,' said Carl. 'I asked Paddy just now. He said it was built in 1862, and they laid the foundation actually on the rock of Athens, so it is pretty safe in case of earthquakes.'

'They don't get earthquakes, do they?' said Loveday nervously.

'Occasionally they have them, but nothing spectacular, I gather, so don't start worrying. I know you. Look, during the Second World War the Germans took the hotel over for their headquarters while they were occupying Greece—they chose it because they knew it was built like a fortress.'

'Oh, it's too elegant to be called a fortress,' Loveday said, her eyes screwed up against the sun so that she could focus better. 'Look, that man on the balcony on the second floor...'

Annis shot a look upward and stiffened in shock. Oh, no! What if he came down here? Made a scene?

'I'm sure I recognise him,' Loveday thought aloud. 'Do you, Carl?'

Carl stared, shook his head. 'Can't say I do. Why, do you think he's a film star?' He grinned teasingly, and his sister pulled a face at him.

'No, I didn't say that! But I know I've seen his face before—and he is rather terrific, wouldn't you say, Annis?' Annis stayed silent, but Loveday didn't mind that, she was sighing romantically. 'I love men who look like that—tall and slim, with black hair and a gorgeous golden tan.'

'Mediterranean men!' Carl said drily. 'He's probably a waiter at the hotel.'

'Don't be silly! In that bathrobe? No, he's a guest, and he must have a huge room to have a balcony that size. He may be a Greek millionaire,' Loveday was inventing wildly now, her eyes dreamy. 'With a big yacht and his own little island off the Greek coast.' She kept her eyes fixed on the watching figure, excitement in her face. 'Look! He's staring back at us! He's looking at me, I'm sure he is! Oh, if only we'd stayed in the hotel last night I might have met him, had dinner with him.'

Carl gave her an amused glance. 'What an imagination you've got!'

His sister turned to glare at him. 'Well, take a look! He's leaning over the balcony, staring—deny that if you can!'

Carl shot a look upward. 'He's staring at you because you've been staring at him.'

Annis was the first to climb into the coach, glad to escape. Loveday and Carl joined her a moment later, and Loveday excitedly said to her, 'Guess what! That guy on the balcony, the one who was staring at me...you know?'

Annis nodded silently, wishing Loveday would stop talking about him, wishing the coach would start so that they could get away from the hotel and any danger of a further confrontation.

'The hotel porter told me who he was...you'll never guess! It was Raphael Leon, the composer!' Loveday was sparkling with pleasure.

Annis forced a look of surprise. 'Really?' she managed huskily.

'You aren't getting a cold, are you?' Loveday asked her, frowning. 'Maybe that's why you had tummy trouble all night. I hope you haven't picked up some bug.'

'No, I'm fine,' Annis said in a level voice. 'Everyone's on the coach, now, why aren't we going? The later it gets, the worse Athens' traffic will be while we're finding our way out of the city.'

'The courier is looking at a map with the driver,' Carl told her. 'I hope that isn't an ominous sign. All we need to enjoy this trip is a driver who doesn't know the way.'

Loveday ignored him. 'Imagine—Raphael Leon in the same hotel!' she said, then gave Annis an impatient look. 'Well, you do know who he is, don't you?'

'Yes,' Annis admitted, keeping her face in profile to the hotel in case he was still on the balcony watching the coach.

'He wrote that wonderful music for the film... whatsit... you know... the sci-fi film. Oh, what was it called...? Everyone was humming it for ages, and the record got into the top ten. What was the film called, though? I remember the music, it goes la la la,' Loveday sang and her brother put his hands over his ears.

'Please! It's too early in the morning for a headache.'

'*Journey to the Furthest Star*,' Annis said tonelessly, and Loveday exclaimed.

'That was it! Did you see it? I did.'

'And didn't understand what it was all about, as I recall,' Carl teased.

'Oh, shut up, you! Well, it was pretty way-out stuff, but the music was utterly fabulous. Apparently, he's a conductor as well as a composer, and he's in Athens to conduct at a concert tonight. Isn't it a pity we're leaving Athens? We could have gone to the concert.' Loveday had that dreamy look again, she was spinning her webs of make-believe. 'Then afterwards we might have had supper back here and he might have come in and we could have asked him to eat with us, and——'

'Oh, do stop it!' Annis broke out hoarsely, and then could have bitten off her tongue as her friends looked round at her in stunned surprise. She felt herself flush and sighed. 'Sorry. I'm sorry, Loveday...it's just...I've got a headache...I didn't mean to snap at you, it just came out.'

'That's OK,' Loveday said amiably, but she was frowning. 'It isn't like you to be so irritable, you're usually so easygoing. You must be ill. Maybe we should ask Paddy to get a doctor when we're in Corinth.'

'I'll see how I feel when we get there,' Annis said hurriedly. The coach started as she was talking, and she leaned back with intense relief, closing her eyes. 'And I think I'll try and snatch some sleep on the way.'

She did not expect to go to sleep, but in fact she did, as the coach jolted through the hills to Thebes, a famous name in ancient Greece, and now a bustling town which served as a market centre for the local farmers. Annis woke up when the coach briefly stopped there so that the passengers could have some coffee.

'How do you feel now?' asked Carl sympathetically, and she smiled at him.

'Fine, thanks. Sorry to have been such a grouch earlier.'

'Listen, at that hour of the morning anyone is entitled to be a grouch!' he said, his hazel eyes warm. She laughed at the remark, which was so typical of him. Carl was a casual, lazy, laid-back young man, but he was also very down-to-earth and sane, and she trusted him and liked him very much. She liked him enough to wish she more than liked him, because that would solve most of her problems, but you couldn't love to order, and she did not love Carl.

They had lunch at a little taverna just outside Corinth, owned, it turned out, by the coach driver's brother-in-law. The meal was simple but delicious: rice-stuffed vine leaves, followed by lamb kebabs and salad with pitta bread, and then honey cakes with fresh grapes picked from the vines growing over the open terrace of the taverna.

As they drank their small cups of very sweet, very strong coffee, Loveday looked out over the sun-hazed landscape and sighed. 'Just think—back at the office now, everyone is slaving away!'

Everyone around them laughed, as much at Loveday's smug expresson as at what she had said, but Annis had a wry look in her blue eyes. She was half wishing she had never come to Greece; she wouldn't have re-opened old wounds which she had thought quite healed.

They visited the famous Corinth canal before driving on to their hotel, and those of them who felt energetic enough later went out for a walk around the ruins of ancient Corinth, while the faint-hearted or the weary stayed in their rooms to rest before dinner.

The following day was very hot, but, armed with sun-hats and even some old-fashioned parasols, they all went sightseeing again to hear a lecture by Paddy on the history of Corinth, given on the site of the market place where St Paul had preached to the Corinthians. Then they had lunch at the hotel, followed by an afternoon free for a siesta, which was becoming a popular idea with some of the older members of the group, or for personal shopping or exploration. Carl, Loveday and Annis went shopping for souvenirs and gifts, and decided to have a quick swim in the hotel pool before going up to rest before dinner. Loveday had bought a new bikini, which she eagerly tried on in their room, only to decide crossly that it was too revealing.

'It's very pretty!' Annis insisted, but Loveday wouldn't be persuaded.

'You go on down. I'll change into my old one,' she muttered, scowling at her reflection.

Annis saw she was hot and irritable, after a very long and tiring day, so she discreetly slipped out of the room and went out to the swimming-pool. It was empty at that hour, most people having had a swim and gone in to change. There was no sign of Carl. Had he changed his mind? wondered Annis, slipping off her flimsy cotton sarong, which she threw across a lounger. She dived into the pool, gasping briefly at the impact of the cool water on her overheated skin, before beginning to swim a few lengths in a lazy fashion. She didn't hear a sound, but suddenly a hand seized her foot and pulled her downwards.

Annis struggled, twisting to face her attacker, and found Carl grinning at her through the blue, sunlit water; he let go and they surfaced together.

'You lunatic!' spluttered Annis.

'I couldn't resist it! Sorry,' Carl said, still laughing. 'Blame my sense of humour.'

'Weird sense of humour!' she retorted. 'Let's see you laugh at this!' and she beat the water with both hands, making a fountain of white spume descend around Carl.

'Now you're asking for it!' said Carl, grabbing her by the waist and pulling her off her feet.

She struggled to get away, but she was laughing, and Carl took no notice as she kicked and writhed; their bodies rolled over and over in the water, like dolphins at play, until a shadow fell over them both, startling Carl into looking up at someone standing on the edge of the pool behind Annis. Carl let go of her, his face suddenly blank, and Annis turned, smiling, expecting to see Loveday standing there.

It wasn't Loveday. It was Raphael Leon, and Annis could see why Carl had gone blank and quiet. Their light-hearted tussle had been watched with implacably hostile eyes.

CHAPTER TWO

CARL recognised him, of course, and muttered, 'Good lord! It's that guy Loveday flipped over!' under his breath, which for some reason made Annis start to laugh almost hysterically. Both men looked at her, Carl with surprise and bewilderment, Raphael with cold, sharp eyes from which she turned away, swimming furiously towards the far end of the pool to give herself time to think.

She hadn't even dreamt that he might follow them here. How had he found them? She was sure she hadn't told him which hotel they would be staying at in Corinth, but then Corinth was not a large town. He had probably seen the name of their tour company on the side of their coach when he had stood on his balcony in Athens the day before, and no doubt he had only had to make a few phone calls to find out where that particular party of tourists was staying in Corinth.

But why had he come after them? She turned on to her back and floated, staring up at the deep blue sky. It was seven o'clock in the evening, and, although it was still bright and very warm, yet the sun was no longer so ferocious and she wasn't afraid of getting sunburn at this time of day. Indeed, she shivered slightly.

What did Raphael intend? There had been bitter hostility in his eyes when they had had that encounter in her hotel bedroom, two days ago. Raphael hated her, she couldn't blind herself to that fact; and whatever motive he had for following her she was under no illusion—it must mean trouble for her.

24

She stiffened, hearing his voice, but couldn't hear what he had said. A pause, then he laughed, and another voice drifted through the evening air—a woman's voice, breathless, excited. Loveday! thought Annis, and hurriedly turned over to swim to the side of the pool and haul herself out of the water.

Carl was already standing on the tiles, talking to his sister and Raphael. None of them noticed Annis padding barefoot towards them, and she paused to pick up her sarong and wind it around her body, then wrung out her long blonde hair, listening intently to the conversation.

'We only found out about the concert the morning we were leaving Athens, but I would have loved to go to it!' Loveday was saying, her face a little flushed and her eyes very bright as she looked up at Raphael. 'I'm a big fan of yours.'

'Thank you,' he murmured with the habitual grace with which he met such remarks. Annis had heard dozens of fans clamouring for his attention, heard them flatter him far more than Loveday was doing, and she recognised that voice, that smile, the mixture of modest courtesy and charm which Loveday apparently found overwhelming, but which was automatic to Raphael by now.

'Do you often conduct abroad?' Carl asked with faint amusement over his sister's starry-eyed excitement.

'Quite often,' Raphael agreed, shrugging. 'I've been on tour in Europe for the past six weeks, for instance.'

'Six weeks!' Carl made a face. 'That must be tiring.'

'Very.' There was dryness in Raphael's voice at this understatement.

Annis stared intently at his razor-edged profile, seeing for the first time the tell-tale signs of weariness which during their barbed exchange in Athens she had missed. There were blueish shadows under his eyes, lines etched around his mouth, a pallor under that deep, golden tan which at first sight made him seem so fit and healthy. Anxiety made her bite her lip. She knew what tours did to him—the constant drain of energy, the need to tighten his nerves to concert pitch, the increasing tension and irritability. The life of a professional musician, with all the demands of creativity, the stress of rehearsal and performance in front of an audience, not to mention the travelling which it entailed, was a severe strain, and Raphael was only a couple of years off forty. How much more could he take without cracking?

'Are you giving a concert in Corinth?' asked Loveday, without being able to hide her eagerness.

'No, my tour ended in Athens,' he coolly said. 'I'm taking a few days' rest.'

'Staying here?'

Annis held her breath. Please, please don't say yes! she thought, but Raphael was nodding.

'I thought I might drive around the Peloponnese, see some of the ancient sites, visit Mycenae, and Argos.'

Loveday was radiant. 'That's what we're doing. There are some empty places on the coach—why don't you join us? We've got a marvellous guide. He knows simply everything about Greek history; he's half-Greek himself. And when we get to the sites we have a local Greek guide to tell us about each place. I feel I'm learning a lot about ancient Greece, and it's fun, too.'

Annis was appalled. The idea of having Raphael on their coach made her blood run cold. Carl didn't look terribly pleased, either. So far the holiday had been an easygoing, friendly affair with the three of them very happy together, but Carl could see that if this famous composer joined their party it would ruin the atmosphere.

Raphael seemed to consider the idea, his head to one side, pushing back a strand of thick black hair with one hand while he thought about it. Annis moved nervously, and he swung round to look at her, his hard, narrowed eyes flicking down her body in a stare that saw everything: her taut features, her loose wet hair, and the way her flimsy cotton sarong clung to her damp body, outlining her breasts, the curve of her bare midriff, the tiny bikini briefs and her long, slim legs. She tensed under that insolent appraisal and saw mockery glitter in his eyes, like sunlight on ice. He knew how disturbed she was by the prospect of his joining the tour, and it appeared to give him some sort of bitter amusement.

'I'm tempted,' he drawled, watching her pale, then he shrugged and looked back at Loveday. 'But actually I've hired a car. Thank you for the offer, though.' He smiled and Annis felt a wave of pure rage mount to her head as she watched the familiar charm of that smile and her friend's flushed reaction. She wasn't angry with Loveday, who had no idea that Raphael was anything but a total stranger to her. Loveday was merely following her female instincts, responding to a highly attractive male in a natural way. No, it wasn't Loveday she wanted to slap. It was Raphael.

'Oh, what a pity,' Loveday said wistfully. 'It would have been such fun, and we would all have loved to have you with us.'

'I would have loved to join you,' he assured her smoothly.

She cheered up, giving him a flirtatious little grin. 'Well, maybe we'll run into you now and then?'

'Oh, I'm sure you will,' he said softly, his mouth twisting, and shot a sideways, taunting glance to see how Annis took that.

She had herself well under control by then, however. Without meeting his stare, she turned towards the hotel, her blonde hair hanging down over her bare, wet shoulders. Loveday noticed her going, and called, 'Annis! Hey! Wait a minute! I want to introduce you to Mr Leon——'

'Raphael,' he interrupted, and Loveday glowed.

'Raphael...' She sighed it, smiling. 'It's such a romantic name. I'm Loveday—and this is my brother, Carl, and my friend, Annis.'

He deliberately held out his hand. 'Hello.' Annis couldn't avoid giving him her own hand.

'Hello,' she said flatly.

His grip was firm and warm, yet she shivered as if his fingers were icy cold, and drew her hand away as soon as she could without being too obvious. He knew, of course—he felt the faint shiver run through her, and he was not surprised when she pulled her hand free a second too soon. His eyes watched her coldly.

'We work together,' Loveday explained. 'And it seemed a good idea to go on holiday together—so much more fun than going away alone, don't you agree? We work in an advertising agency—you may have heard of it. Quayland, Corris and Worth. That's us—Worth, I mean—that was my uncle, Dan Worth, one of the founding partners. Our agency handles some big accounts; you'll have read some of our stuff in newspapers and magazines. Do you drive the new Orage car? We handled that campaign. I'm an artist, and Carl writes copy—he's done some very well-known slogans—but I don't think we've ever run a campaign for an orchestra. That would be quite a challenge, wouldn't it, Carl?'

Loveday was chattering, not because she was nervous but because she was trying to keep him there, stop him walking away. Annis looked at her wryly. She understood how Loveday felt. He was the sort of man who made women go weak at the knees. Even if he hadn't been famous, he would still have made women flip because he was intensely male and a challenge to their femininity.

She had seen it happen before, many times, and she didn't enjoy watching it happen to Loveday. She wished she could warn her, but how could she without betraying herself?

Raphael looked at her. 'What do you do in this advertising agency?' he asked with an edge of sarcasm to his voice.

'I'm a secretary,' she said shortly, then looked at Loveday. 'I'm going in to get dressed for dinner; it's getting late.'

She didn't wait for an answer but walked away, head up, back straight, aware of being watched but not looking back. In her room, she showered, blow-dried her hair, dressed and made up her face with slow precision, to stop herself thinking, but it didn't work. Her head was buzzing with anxious questions.

Raphael had pursued her here for some motive—presumably to hurt her, to get some sort of revenge for the way she had hurt him—but what could he do?

He could make life difficult, he could torment her, keep her on tenterhooks, wondering exactly what he was going to do—but Annis couldn't believe he would take such a petty revenge. That hadn't been Raphael's nature; he could be arrogant at times, he could domineer, ride roughshod over the musicians he worked with in the attempt to get their best work out of them, but he was also deeply sensitive, and he could be very gentle. She could never remember him being spiteful or malicious.

But he was here, in the same hotel—so what was he up to? She jumped as someone knocked on the door, staring at it, transfixed.

'Annis, open up!' Loveday called and Annis relaxed, closing her eyes for an instant before hurrying to the door.

'Sorry, I left my key in here,' Loveday apologised. 'Look at the time! I must rush or I'll be late for dinner.' She went into the bathroom and shut the door, but went on talking through it, her voice raised. 'Pity we won't be able to sit with Raphael at dinner. Wasn't it incredible, meeting up with him here? After seeing him in Athens like that? Isn't he gorgeous, Annis? Now, hands off—he's mine, I saw him first. Do you think he likes me? After you'd gone, Carl went in to change, but Raphael stayed out by the pool with me. That's why I'm so late; he kept asking me questions.'

Annis stood very still, frowning. 'Questions?' she asked, but Loveday was showering now and didn't hear above the rush of water. She didn't emerge from the bathroom for several minutes. When she did come out, wrapped in a big white bathtowel, her wet hair coiling around her pink face, Annis asked again, 'Questions about what?' trying to look casual, to smile.

'Where's that hairdrier?' Loveday asked, opening a drawer and rummaging about. 'Oh, here it is...' She switched it on and began to blow-dry her thick red hair, using a brush to put the wave back into it. Above the noise of the electric motor, she yelled, 'What did you say?' and Annis repeated her question in a flat voice.

Loveday shrugged. 'Oh, all sorts of things—he seemed really interested in me, in the firm, in Carl and you. And he listened to everything I said. You know the way people pretend, being polite, but not really taking in a word? Well, he really listened!' Loveday put down the hairdrier and considered her reflection in the dressing-table mirror. 'How does that look? OK?'

'It looks great,' Annis said, feeling cold. Raphael had been asking questions. And listening to the answers. What was he up to? She seriously began to wonder if she ought to leave at once, fly back to London. What excuse could she give? Invent an illness? She knew she wasn't up to faking a serious illness. A headache, tummy ache…those she could manage to fake, but nothing more alarming than that, and if she did they would call a local doctor and he would immediately pronounce her a phoney.

Loveday went to the wardrobe and began pulling out dresses. 'Oh, what shall I wear?' she wailed. 'I want to knock him cold. What do I look great in, Annis?'

'That green silk,' said Annis from the door. 'I'm going down now. See you later.' She couldn't stand listening any longer to her friend rhapsodising about Raphael, or speculating as to whether or not he fancied her.

Down in the bar, she joined a group of their coach party, accepted a glass of Greek retsina, the smoky, resinated white wine she had grown to enjoy, and sat with them, listening rather than talking.

When they went into the dining-room, Annis went with them because she was afraid of being alone in case Raphael came along. Loveday and Carl arrived a few moments later, and the special set dinner was served. The rest of the guests in the dining-room could eat off the menu, but the coach party were quite separate. Their meal was good, though: a lemony chicken soup, followed by a macaroni and meat dish with a flavour like spaghetti bolognese, and then green figs or ice-cream. Annis chose the figs; they were delicious. After their tiny cups of incredibly strong, sweet coffee, they all went out to sit around the floodlit pool, drinking Greek brandy and watching the moon shine down over the darkened garden.

There was no sign of Raphael, as Loveday kept saying. 'Maybe he's gone to bed early—the guy must have been exhausted!' Carl suggested impatiently. 'Or maybe he's gone out somewhere, having dinner with friends—he probably knows people around here, the man is world-famous! In fact, I can't understand what he's doing in this hotel. I would have thought he would stay somewhere very grand and expensive.' He got up. 'I'm going to play table tennis, work off some of that dinner—coming, girls?'

Loveday was on her feet at once, but Annis shook her head. 'I feel sleepy, I'm going to bed in a moment.'

'I'll sneak in quietly when I come,' promised Loveday.

'I hope you've got your key this time!'

Loveday laughed. 'Yes, here it is!' She dangled it from a finger, then pushed it into her little silver purse. 'I'll try not to wake you up.'

When they had gone, Annis got up too, but it was really still early for bed so she took a stroll through the hotel gardens, along maze-like little gravelled paths between flower-beds and low walls swagged with starry, purple wisteria, listening to the whirr of the cicadas in the trees, breathing the scent of flowers. From around the pool came laughter, voices, from the hotel, music, but under the trees there was a calming silence, until she turned a corner in the path and saw a dark shape looming in front of her.

She gave an involuntary gasp of alarm, and the shape moved, materialising from the shadows of the tree above it. It was Raphael, in evening dress, his white shirt gleaming in the darkness.

'All alone?' he asked with chilling mockery. 'Where's the boyfriend? And don't tell me he isn't your boyfriend, because his chatty sister has already confided how much she hopes you'll marry him.'

'I'm sure she didn't say any such thing!' Loveday had never breathed a word about wanting her to marry Carl. Come to that, Carl had never shown any sign of asking her. Their relationship was friendly; they weren't lovers.

'Did you warn her not to?' The question came like a dagger, sharp and tipped with poison.

'No!' Her eyes darkened with temper, she felt like hitting him.

'No,' he conceded very softly, and a shiver ran down her back at the tone. 'They don't know very much about you at all, do they? They don't even know we've met before. I wonder what they would think if they found out.'

The veiled threat made her even angrier. 'Don't try to blackmail me! What are you doing here, anyway? You followed me here, didn't you? What do you think you're doing? Why don't you go back to Athens and fly home?' Her voice shook and she almost yelled at him. 'Fly anywhere, but leave me alone!'

She turned to flee, but at that instant a moth blundered out of the dark shadows into the light. She was afraid of moths, a primitive, irrational fear she had had since childhood. The soft, furry wings brushed her face, and she cried out, shuddering with horror.

'What's the matter?' Raphael moved so fast that he had an arm around her before she knew what was happening.

'A...a moth...' she muttered, trying to push him away, and shaking even more while he was so close.

'A moth?' he said, his arm immovable, and took hold of her chin, forcing her head back so that the moonlight fell on it and showed him her pale features, her wide eyes and quivering lips. 'Yes, I remember you were always scared of moths.'

She tried to jerk her head aside, afraid of that probing stare. 'Let go, Raphael! I must go in, it's getting late.'

'Later than you think,' he said oddly, and she didn't like the way he said it.

She wouldn't let him see how much he was disturbing her, though. Her blue eyes spat defiance at him. 'Will you stop trying to get at me? OK, I don't like moths, but neither do lots of perfectly sane and sensible people. And don't think you can bully or blackmail me by threatening to tell Carl and Loveday we knew each other before, either! I really don't care if you tell them or not. I've done nothing to be ashamed of! I changed my mind about you, but that isn't a crime.'

'Shut up!' he bit out, the tanned skin drawn tightly over his cheekbones.

A quiver of panic ran through her as she met his angry eyes. She could see she had touched on a nerve and she bit her lip. More gently, she said, 'Oh, Raphael, I'm sorry it ended that way. I'm sorry if you got hurt; it was the last thing I wanted to do—hurt you. I know that's a cliché, but I'm not using it glibly, it happens to be true. I really didn't want to hurt you, but I had no choice.'

'Why?' he asked at once, watching her with those intent, fixed eyes.

'This isn't doing any good, Raphael,' she said uneasily. 'Please…can we go back into the hotel? There's no point in a post-mortem, don't you see that? It was over two years ago...'

'Not for me!'

Annis looked into his face in unguarded shock, wondering what exactly that meant—was he saying he still loved her? Her heart seemed to stop, then it went on much faster. But that was not how love looked—that was hatred in his eyes, in the aggressive tension of his lean body, and she gave a long, weary sigh. 'Please, Raphael... I've said I'm sorry and I meant it, believe it. Can't you just let it go?'

'No, damn you!' he ground out between his teeth. His skin was dark red, his eyes glittered. She should have guessed he would take it like this, she realised numbly. Maybe that was one reason why she hadn't told him, why she had sent that letter and vanished. She had been afraid to face him, afraid of an explosive reaction. There had always been an all-or-nothing element in Raphael's character; he was a perfectionist, ready to go to any trouble to achieve what he wanted, obsessive, dedicated. That was what made him a highly respected conductor and composer.

But there was always a flip side to any virtue, and this was the other side of Raphael's creative intensity. He couldn't shrug off the past; he had brooded on it all this time.

'I can't let it go because I don't know why you left me,' he muttered. 'And until I do, I shan't be able to forget you. There's too much unfinished business between us. It nags away at me night and day. I keep wondering why... why...'

'Raphael, you mustn't,' she whispered, pain in her voice, looking up at him almost pleadingly.

He looked down, his face hard, clenched in male aggression; then suddenly he caught her face between his hands, his own head coming down towards her.

'No!' she groaned, panic flaring, turning and twisting to evade his searching mouth.

'Yes,' he said thickly. 'There's something I have to know!' and his lips closed over hers. Annis was lost from the moment their mouths met; her mind submerged be-

neath crashing waves of intense pleasure. It was a long
time since any man had held her in his arms like this,
kissed her with passion. It was a shock; her body
quivered in helpless reaction. Raphael had both arms
around her, he was pulling her closer and closer, their
bodies merging into one in the black shadows of the trees.
He pulled the Spanish combs out of her carefully dressed
hair and it tumbled down her back in silky blonde dis-
order. He ran his fingers through the strands, caressed
the nape of her neck, let his hand slide downwards to
cup her breast, and she shook with sensual need, her
whole body on fire.

Somewhere at the back of her mind she knew this was
madness and she would regret it, but how could she listen
to that little warning voice when desire was singing
through her body, silencing every other sound?

What at last Raphael lifted his head, they were both
breathing raggedly. He looked at her in silence, his face
deeply flushed, and she stared back, eyes drowsy, not
capable of thought.

'You couldn't kiss me like that, and be indifferent,'
Raphael said huskily, and she came back to her senses,
realising how reckless and stupid she had been. She
should never have let him get near her, never have let
him touch her. What on earth could she say now?

'I never said I didn't enjoy it when we made love!'
she whispered, at last. 'I've always been attracted to
you—you're very sexy. But finding a man sexy isn't a
good enough reason for getting married, is it? There has
to be more than that. Marriage is a whole way of life,
a total commitment—and I'm not ready to make it.'

'You were!' he said fiercely, shaking her. 'You were,
Annis! You were as happy about getting married as I
was; there weren't any doubts for either of us until I
went on that last tour. I was only away a month—but

when I got back you were gone and that letter was waiting for me. What happened? There has to be a reason. What happened while I was away?'

'I keep telling you,' Annis desperately said. 'I changed my mind about marrying you. That's all.'

'There's more to it than that—there has to be!' Raphael watched her searchingly, trying to decipher the riddle of her mind from studying her face. 'What about this other man? What did he mean to you? You said you'd found someone else. When I talked to your friend Loveday, it was obvious that you hadn't met her brother until long after you ran out on me, so it must have been some other guy you left me for—where is he now? And if you walked out on me for him, why didn't you marry him? Or did you? Is he still around? Or do you pick men up and drop them again all the time? Is that it?'

She was too tired to argue any more. 'Yes, that's it,' she said. 'You've hit the nail on the head. I'm sorry, but there's nothing more to say. I just want to go back to my room.'

Her weary tone appeared to be a red rag to a bull. He glowered at her, eyes dark. 'You collect men, and when you're tired of your latest toy you drop him and go and find a new one?'

The tone of his voice was an insult; it was like being hit in the face. She took a long breath before she could answer. 'Why don't you go back to London, and forget we ever met, Raphael? This sort of insult-swapping isn't going to get either of us anywhere. Stop it now, for heaven's sake! You're just wasting time and energy, and I can't put up with much more of it. I've had enough.'

He laughed bitterly. 'Oh, you've had enough, have you?'

His hands bit into her shoulders; he shook her, those grey eyes glittering like the points of spears, and she really became frightened as she stared back fixedly. There was danger in the air; there was violence in his face and she no longer felt she knew him. During the months when they were together, wildly in love and so happy that the rest of the world hardly seemed to exist for them, Raphael had been funny, charming, tender, kind—a warm and thoughtful lover with whom she felt totally secure. She didn't know this man shaking her and looking at her as if he wanted to kill her. He was a stranger, whom she found inhabiting the body of the man she had once loved more than anyone else in the world.

'Listen to me carefully, Annis!' he said, bending towards her with threat in every line of his body. 'I've got two years behind me, two years of wondering what the hell went wrong and what sort of guy took you away from me and whether he was that much better in bed than I am! And you say you've had enough? You've got a long way to go before you catch up on the agony you put me through, and, believe me, Annis, I haven't even started on you yet.'

She looked at him, turning white. When she had left him, she had known it would be a shock, that he would be hurt and angry—but she hadn't imagined that he would be put through anything so traumatic that he wouldn't get over it in a matter of weeks or months. He would be too busy to miss her much, she had thought, knowing his lifestyle. Raphael's work was his real love; in fact, it was almost everything in his life, occupying most of his waking hours, and most of his thoughts. In the pursuit of his career Raphael travelled the world, and everywhere he went there were bound to be women throwing themselves at him. There would be plenty of female fans eager to comfort him and help him forget her.

'I'm——' she began shakily, and he interrupted, his voice harsh.

'Don't say you're sorry again, or I'll hit you!'

She trembled, and he let go of her. Annis didn't wait to hear if he had anything else to say. She fled, away from the dark shadows and the moonlit garden, back to the bright lights and noise of the crowded hotel, where it was much safer.

Loveday was in their room, in a shortie nightie, brushing her red hair in front of the dressing-table mirror. 'Where on earth have you been?' she demanded as soon as Annis opened the door, swinging round to stare accusingly at her. 'You said you were coming to bed hours ago!'

'It was so warm that I went for a walk,' said Annis huskily, still breathing much too fast and aware that she was flushed and shaky. She grabbed up her own night-dress and made hurriedly for the bathroom before Loveday could notice the state she was in.

'Who with?' Loveday was kidding; she laughed as she said it. Annis answered as lightly, pretending to laugh, but kept her back turned so that her friend could not glimpse her face.

'All by myself in the moonlight.'

'What a waste of a moon!' said Loveday as Annis shut the door on her. She needed to shower, she was so hot and on edge, and the clean, cool needles of water were heavenly on her overheated skin. She stood under the spray, eyes closed, gradually breathing slower and more calmly, trying not to think about Raphael, but failing miserably because her mind was full of images of him kissing her in the shadow of the trees. She could even smell the perfume of the flowers, hear the cicadas.

Well, of course she could hear them! she impatiently told herself. She had heard them ever since she had come to Greece. They were whirring away out there now, a constant, sealike murmur all night, in the rough-barked pines and crooked olive trees surrounding the hotel. Before the hotel was built there had been a little farm-house here, in the middle of an olive grove, and some of the remaining trees were very old. Their twisted branches still bore those silvery, dancing leaves, but rarely any olives.

She turned off the shower, dried herself briefly, put on her nightdress and inspected her reflection to make sure that she looked quite normal now, then went out to join Loveday, who was in bed reading a paperback.

Annis yawned deliberately as she climbed into bed, afraid her friend would ask questions she did not want to answer. 'I'm too tired to read tonight.'

'Oh, good—so am I.' Loveday turned out the light, and they both settled down to sleep.

They had to be up very early next day to eat a quick breakfast and then set out on a long coach trip to Mycenae and other archaeological sites in the Peloponnese. The morning, as usual, was the coolest part of the day; blueish shadows of trees lay on the roads as they drove away from Corinth and, as the sun rose higher and the shadows vanished, the smell of thyme and gorse grew stronger in the hills. Annis sat by the window, staring out at the sunburnt landscape. The sky was deep blue; the sun hurt her eyes. The air-conditioning in the coach barely seemed to stir the air, and some of the older members of the group were fanning themselves.

Loveday kept talking about Raphael. They hadn't seen him at breakfast. 'I hope he hasn't moved on!' Loveday said, and Annis prayed fervently that he had.

Their coach let them down at the bottom of the little slope leading up to the Lion Gate of the ancient city of Mycenae, and they straggled up to it behind their courier and the Greek guide, who was giving them a running lecture on the history of the city. Carl took snap after snap, persuading the two girls to pose as the human elements of his photographs, in front of the massive stones of the Lion Gate, in front of the little guard room just inside the Gate, and standing on the broken walls of the citadel so that Carl could get in a breathtaking vista of the green and brown valleys and the purple-hazed hills behind them.

'The view is magnificent,' Loveday said, her red hair whipped about by the wind on those heights. Under her arm, she had the sketchbook she took everywhere with her. She sat down on a wall and began sketching; Annis watched her for a few moments and then wandered off to listen to the guide telling their party about the graves of Agamemnon and Clytemnestra.

'But, of course, although when they were first discovered this was the immediate conclusion of Schliemann, we know far more about Greek history now, and we realise that the dating was quite wrong, and...'

Annis strolled on, fanning herself with her white straw hat. The heat was unbearable out in the sun; she wanted to find some shade. Carl was leaping about like a goat, taking photos of everything he saw. Loveday was still sketching, the guide still talking. Annis sat down near a wall, out of the sun, and closed her eyes.

'You OK?'

She opened her eyes again, smiling at Carl, who was bending over her with concern in his face. 'I'm fine,' she said. 'It's just so hot!'

'You look cool enough in that cotton dress! Blue is definitely your colour.'

'It's a cold colour, though,' she said, looking down at the simple little dress she wore—tiny cap sleeves, a scooped neckline and tight waist. It emphasised her slender figure but she felt that the ice-blue cotton was rather too pale.

'Suits you,' Carl said, and she wondered if that was a compliment. 'Smile,' he added, taking yet another snap of her, then extended his hand to help her to her feet. 'We're off now, down to see the Beehive Tombs. Have you ever thought how much death comes into archaeology? It's all graves and tombs and funerary objects. Quite creepy, really.' He slid an arm around her waist as she tripped on a loose stone going down the hill from the Lion Gate. 'Careful! You don't want to break an ankle and ruin the trip.'

They found Loveday at the bottom of the hill, flushed and bright-eyed. 'Guess who I just saw?' she burst out the minute they were in earshot.

Carl pulled a face. 'Not him again! Is he following us around?'

Loveday laughed delightedly. 'Maybe he is!' The idea was clearly flattering.

Annis said nothing, she just stared at a large, rather old but well-kept white car which was driving past at that moment. Raphael was at the wheel. He flicked a look sideways at that instant, met her eyes, then looked away again, but not before she had seen the icy implacability of his stare. Annis shivered, in spite of the heat of the sun. It wasn't pleasant to feel yourself the focus of so much concentrated enmity.

The coach party went on to the 'beehive' tombs, built below the hill and outside the city walls. The architects and builders had amazing skill; the massive, cyclopean stones had been fitted together perfectly, as their guide pointed out at some length. The party was shepherded down into the darkness of the tombs so that they could admire the construction of the domed roof.

'I hate this!' Loveday suddenly said, and rushed out.

Annis looked around anxiously. 'What's wrong with her? Is she ill?' she asked Carl, who shook his head ruefully.

'A touch of claustrophobia, I expect. I'll go and make sure she's OK.'

'I'll come, too,' Annis said, but he told her to stay and listen to the guide, who was taking their party into the inner tomb.

Annis followed in time to see the guide strike a match to illuminate the dark interior, then the light went out and the party groped their way out again, with a few nervous giggles. Annis waited until they were all out before she turned to go, and then bumped into someone in the dark.

'Sorry,' she began and then stopped as her nerve-ends bristled in recognition. She didn't know how she knew who it was, because he hadn't spoken and she couldn't see anything of him, but every instinct she possessed was giving a warning.

'I told you to stop saying that!' Raphael muttered.

She tried to slide past him but he caught hold of her shoulders and slammed her backwards, against the stone walls. Annis gave a stifled cry of shock. 'Don't!'

He put his face against hers, his lips touching her mouth, and whispered thickly, 'I've made up my mind. You're leaving this coach party tonight. You're coming with me.'

'No,' she breathed, turning her head away, shuddering.

'I'm not watching you flirting with Carl Worth any more. You aren't staying with this tour. Either do as I tell you or——' He broke off as there was a sound of voices, footsteps. Another party had arrived, another guide was talking in that well-rehearsed sing-song.

'And here we have the inner tomb.' He struck a match, shedding a flickering light around the stone walls, and

Annis tore herself out of Raphael's grip and ran to catch up with her own group, who had by now emerged into the sun. Carl and Loveday were already in the coach. Loveday gave her a wry grin as she joined them.

'Stupid of me, sorry to be such an idiot—but I can't stand dark, underground places. I could never go pot-holing! I even hate the London Tube!'

'It was rather creepy in there,' Annis said, sitting down, her eyes on the white Mercedes into which Raphael was climbing at that moment. She bit her lip. What had he been about to say when that other group of tourists arrived? She must either do as he said, or... what?

CHAPTER THREE

'YOU'VE been preoccupied all day!' Carl said to Annis that night at dinner. 'Is anything wrong?'

She gave him a quick, wary look, wondering what he had noticed or overheard. 'No, nothing's wrong—why?'

'When we left London, you were so excited about this trip, but you've gone very quiet since...' He frowned, obviously thinking back. 'Since we left Athens. Yes, you've been like this since the morning we left Athens. Aren't you well? Is that it? Is this heat too much for you?'

She met his concerned, friendly eyes, and smiled back gratefully. 'A little, yes. It seems to be getting hotter, too.'

'Yes, I thought that myself. Very close this evening— I hate humid weather, and with your skin you must be careful in the sun.'

'I always wear a hat.'

'I've noticed, very sensible.' Carl fanned himself with his table napkin. 'And this is only the beginning of June—what on earth is it like here in July?'

'Hotter!' Annis laughed and across the room suddenly found herself looking into hard, grey eyes. She looked away quickly, a pulse beating fast in her throat. He had only just walked into the dining-room; she would have been aware of him if he had been there earlier. When she herself first arrived, she had flicked her eyes around the room and slackened in relief when she was sure he was not there, and his absence had made it poss-

ible to relax, to eat her dinner and talk to the others at
her long table without her attention wandering elsewhere.

'We should have come in the spring,' Carl said, and
she absently agreed without having really listened.

Someone else spoke to her and she answered, nodding,
barely aware of what she was saying. Then Loveday
leaned over from the other side of the table, eyes alight.

'He's here!' she whispered. 'By the door! Look! Oh,
I hope they put him at a table near us!'

Annis made a general noise of agreement without
looking towards Raphael, and then ate some more lemon
mousse to keep herself occupied and hide her urgent
desire for Raphael to sit a long way away.

She did not need to watch him to find out where he
was going to be seated; Loveday kept up a running commentary in an excited murmur.

'The head waiter's taking him to the window
table...no, he doesn't want to sit there! He's shaking
his head, and looking round the room. Oh, he's looking
this way. He's seen that empty table next to us...
he——'

'Do shut up, Loveday!' Carl said crossly. 'You sound
like someone doing a commentary on Wimbledon!'

'He's coming over here!' Loveday said, dropping her
napkin. She bent down to pick it up. Annis concentrated
on her plate, on the last sliver of delicate pale yellow
mousse. She knew Raphael was standing beside their
table now; she heard Loveday's breathless voice. 'Oh,
thank you. Clumsy of me. I'm always dropping something. How are you enjoying your holiday? Seeing all
the sights?'

'Some of them,' Raphael drawled coolly. 'Good
evening.' The pitch of his voice told Annis that he was
speaking across the table to her and Carl, and she heard
Carl answer politely, without enthusiasm.

'Good evening.'

Annis pretended not to have heard. She didn't look up. Loveday claimed his attention a second later with more of her headlong, eager talk.

'Isn't it hot tonight? Thank heavens the hotel has a pool—I don't know how we would survive if it didn't. We haven't seen you in the pool yet. Don't you swim?'

'Yes, but you haven't been around when I've been in the pool,' Raphael said. 'So this is your last night here? You move on tomorrow?'

'Yes, to spend a few days by the sea, and get in some sunbathing and swimming before we go home. What about you?'

'I haven't made up my mind what I'm going to do next,' Raphael said, and Annis heard a menacing note in his voice and looked up then, her blue eyes wide. He was watching her; their eyes met and she felt her stomach clench with apprehension. What had he meant in Mycenae that morning? Either she left the coach party and went with him, or... or what?

With most men you could dismiss the threat as mere bluff, but Raphael had always had that element of danger, a dark vein of his character buried beneath the charm everyone else saw. He was too unpredictable for it to be wise to shrug off what he had said.

'Well, I hope you'll be staying to watch the Greek dancing after dinner,' Loveday said hopefully. 'Tonight is cabaret night, and they've promised us all sorts of entertainment.'

He laughed. 'Yes, I know—they asked me if I would play——'

'Oh, please do! I'd love to hear you playing some of your own music!' Loveday broke in with flattering eagerness.

'That's very kind,' Raphael said drily. 'I'm sorry, but I'm on holiday—playing the piano is what I do to earn my daily bread!'

Loveday didn't hide her disappointment. 'Oh, well, of course I understand, but it is a pity, isn't it, Annis? We would have been thrilled.' Hearing nothing from Annis, she kicked her under the table, and Annis looked up again and nodded obediently.

'Yes.'

Raphael studied her with wry amusement in his eyes. 'You really want me to play for you?'

She understood the note in his voice, the mocking look in his eyes. He was making it personal; he wouldn't play for Loveday, but if she begged him to he would play for her.

Loveday was sparkling. 'We'd be over the moon, wouldn't we, Annis?' She didn't understand, of course; how could she? She probably thought that he was simply being swayed by the fact that it wasn't just one person who wanted him to play, that there were others in their party who were dying to hear him.

Annis looked at her friend, and then at Raphael, pugnacity coming into her blue eyes. Why shouldn't Loveday get her wish? 'Yes, please play for us,' she said sweetly, and his mouth twisted.

'Only if you choose the music for me and come and turn the pages while I play.'

Her eyes flashed. She might have known he wouldn't do it just because she asked!

He didn't wait for her to answer; he turned away and sat down at his table, began to study the menu, while Loveday looked at her indignantly, very pink in the face and her red hair looking more fiery than ever. Loveday had a temper to go with her red hair, but it exploded rapidly and died again as soon.

'Hey, what's going on? Have you got your eye on him? I saw him first, he's mine! Butt out, Annis.'

'You kept dragging me into the discussion, I didn't ask to get involved,' Annis said, accepting a cup of the strong, sweet coffee the waiter was bringing round.

'I didn't mean you to start flirting with him, though!'

'I wasn't flirting!' Annis had flushed angrily, afraid that Raphael was able to hear this muttered argument.

'Hmm,' Loveday said, eyeing her sideways. 'Well, I'll believe you this time. I know men usually flip over your blonde hair and blue eyes, especially Mediterranean men. Why do men go for blondes in such a big way? Someone ought to do a psychological study of it. I'm seriously thinking of dyeing my hair blonde. Now, look—I'll choose the music and turn the pages for him. You stay with Carl, and make it clear you aren't interested, OK? If he thinks Carl is your boyfriend, he won't make an issue of it.'

'Thanks,' Carl said wryly, and Annis smiled at him. 'She uses us both shamelessly, doesn't she?'

'Shameless is exactly the word I was looking for! But I don't mind being your boyfriend for tonight, Annis.' He grinned. 'How realistic do we have to be, Loveday? A little kissing and cuddling in a corner? Count me in!'

'Idiot,' his sister said affectionately. 'Just so long as you give Raphael Leon the idea that Annis is spoken for!'

Annis watched the black head at the next table, wondering how he would react to Loveday's plans. She had an uneasy feeling that Loveday wasn't going to get things all her own way for once. They had finished their coffee now; she got up and the others joined her as she moved towards the door. The cabaret was not to begin for an hour, to give everyone time to finish dinner. Most of the coach party had drifted out to sit by the pool, so Annis,

Loveday and Carl went out into the humid evening air and sat with them, talking about what they had seen that day and how eager they all were to get to the seaside and enjoy a few days of lazy sunbathing on the beach after their tiring sightseeing.

The sun was down and the moon and stars out by the time they moved back indoors to watch the cabaret. Annis was tempted to escape by going to bed, but she was afraid Raphael might follow her up there. Loveday chose a table beside the little square of parquet flooring which served as a dance-floor, and Annis sat down between her and Carl, praying that another member of their group would take the empty fourth chair. Someone did come up to claim it, but Loveday promptly said, 'We're keeping that for someone, sorry!'

'Who are we keeping it for?' Carl enquired with sarcasm in his voice. 'Or can I guess? He won't want to sit with us, Loveday! Stop chasing the poor guy.'

His sister went red and glared. 'I am not chasing him! He's on his own, and he looks lonely, that's all.'

Carl gave a hollow laugh. 'Oh, sure! Did you hear that, Annis? He looks lonely and she isn't chasing him, she's just being kind to the guy.'

Annis didn't want to get into that family argument; she watched the little local band setting up their instruments. A few minutes later, the entertainment began with cheerful Greek dancing. The waiters leapt into the room in national costume and began whirling around the floor, stamping their feet and singing with more gusto than musical ability, exhorting everyone to clap their hands and stamp their feet in time to the music.

After this first dance, they were given a brief explanation of the origins of Greek dancing and then one of the dancers did a slow motion version of a dance so that they could see exactly how it was done, then they were all invited to come on to the floor and learn the simple steps.

'Come on!' Carl said, pulling Annis and Loveday to their feet. On the floor, they all linked arms and began dancing with a great deal of laughter and enjoyment, weaving their way around the room in a long chain, in and out between the tables, pulling reluctant members of the audience to their feet to join them.

Raphael came into the room and stood watching them. Annis gave him one quick glance, then looked away, her nerve-endings prickling. She wished she knew what he was thinking, but his shuttered face told her nothing except that she could expect trouble.

Loveday had seen him, too; as they all swept past him she let go of Annis, put out a hand and caught hold of Raphael, pulling him along with them. He smiled at her, then turned his head and looked at Annis through lowered lids, his hand extended to her. She had no option but to take it or break the chain. His cool fingers tightened on hers and she felt a shiver run down her back at the contact. His curling mouth held satisfaction; he had felt her tremble and was pleased by the reaction.

He watched for every tiny sign of awareness, she thought bleakly, and fed on it. The more she tried to evade, the more she betrayed weakness, the more he pursued. If she could only convince him she was indifferent, he would probably leave her alone. He didn't love her; he hated her. The hunger in his eyes was to see her get hurt, the way she had hurt him, and how could she blame him for that? It was a human instinct, to desire revenge, one which civilised societies outlawed but could never quite tame.

Raphael was of Latin descent; he had an English mother, but his father was Spanish and he had grown up in Spain, been educated there, although he had learnt fluent English from his mother, and indeed had done a postgraduate course at Oxford after taking a degree in languages and music in Madrid. He came from a very different culture, one with a wilder side to it than one found in colder climes. His instincts were more extreme, more explosive, and that had fascinated Annis when they first met. She had been endlessly curious about the strangeness in him, the passion, the darkness and emotional power; one heard it in his music, one saw it in his eyes.

Now, it disturbed her, frightened her, because it made him impossible to fathom, dangerously unpredictable. She kept remembering the way he had looked at her, the tone of his voice when he'd said, 'Either do as I tell you or...' Or what? She wished she knew, but she wouldn't, couldn't ask him, because she was afraid of the answer.

The Greek dancing ended a moment later, and they all broke up, clapping and laughing. The Greek waiters took their bow again, then ran off, smiling, and the band began to play a modern waltz. Most of the guests drifted off the floor, a few danced.

Raphael caught Annis's hand as she hurriedly turned away. She looked up in shock when she felt his arm go round her waist.

For a second she really thought he meant to make love to her here, on the dance-floor, in front of everyone, and her mind went haywire. She blushed hotly, trembling, resisting him, the pupils of her blue eyes dilating with fear, and Raphael stared down at her, his eyes mocking.

'Careful, Annis!' he whispered. 'Your boyfriend is going to notice the effect I have on you soon, and start wondering what it means.'

She stiffened, looking down, even more alarmed by the implication of what he'd said, and without waiting for her to answer he swept her in among the other dancing couples. Annis was so disturbed that she couldn't remember how to dance a waltz; she stumbled as he swung her round, and had to cling to him to keep her balance. His arm tightened on her waist, his fingers tightened on her captive hand, he drew her closer, their bodies touching from the shoulder downwards, so that she felt every movement he made.

'You aren't leaving with them tomorrow, you know,' he murmured, his mouth moving against her ear, and she couldn't stop the involuntary quiver of arousal that contact caused. Her whole body was aroused: her breasts ached with heated blood; her heart beat much too fast; her legs were trembling as he moved against her in that intimate embrace.

She had to stop thinking about the way he was holding her, touching her; she had to break out of the trance she was sinkng into. She muttered, 'I *am* going!' and felt the angry tension in the body so close to her own.

'You're coming with me!'

'I won't be bullied into it, so stop threatening me!' she muttered, aware of the people all around them, of ears intent on picking up their whispers.

He swung her in a full circle, her feet leaving the ground and her full skirt flaring out around her legs. The other dancers watched, smiling, quite unaware of Raphael's rage, the violence expressed in lifting her up and swinging her round until she was almost dizzy.

Raphael put her on her feet again, and she swayed against him, her head still going round. He bent his head and his mouth savagely fastened on her lips; it was a brief kiss, but it was like being branded with a hot iron, and Annis was shaking when it was over.

She heard people laughing around them—a few people even clapped, as though they thought the kiss and the way Raphael had whirled her off her feet had all been part of the entertainment, a joke for public consumption. Annis was too dazed and angry to think about other people; she had enough problems thinking about herself and wondering what she was going to do about Raphael.

A moment later, the music stopped with a drum roll and she pulled away from Raphael, evaded his hand as he tried to catch hold of her again, and hurried off the dance-floor. She couldn't go back to the table; she couldn't face her friends just yet. She could imagine how Loveday was going to look at her, eyes accusing. She went, instead, to the ladies' powder-room, found it, to her great relief, empty, and sank on to a pink velvet chair in front of one of the mirrors, staring at her own reflection, biting her lower lip to stop herself bursting into tears. At any minute, someone might come in and if she was crying it would cause a lot of talk.

Raphael was driving her crazy. What on earth was she to do about it? If she went on with the coach party and he followed them, it would be impossible to hide the fact that he was pursuing her. Loveday was going to be very jealous and suspicious, she was going to think Annis had deliberately tried to steal him from her, and the only way to explain why Raphael was following her was to tell Loveday about the past, and she could not bear to talk about all that. If she didn't, though, sooner or later Raphael would probably tell them the whole story, and they would realise how she had lied to them. It would wreck their friendship, and make her job with the advertising agency impossible. She would have to move on again, start building up another life, somewhere else, and she felt weary at the very thought of that. She hated change. She had taken a long time to get used to living in London, and her new job.

The door opened and she sat up, fumbling with her bag to get out her cosmetic bag, switching on a bright smile ready for whoever entered. The smile faltered and vanished as she realised it was Loveday.

'I'm not surprised you're hiding in here!' Loveday burst out, glaring. 'What an exhibition! Dancing cheek to cheek, clinging to him like a boa constrictor! And then that kiss!' She paused, breathing noisily, her face very pink and her hazel eyes green with rage.

'I'm s——' Annis began, and Loveday interrupted sharply.

'Don't you dare say you're sorry! You know you don't mean it, any more than you meant it when you said you weren't interested in him. I knew you were after him too, but you kept insisting that you weren't. Don't pretend any more. If you've fallen for him, you can't help it, I suppose, but you might at least have been honest about it.'

Annis winced at the contempt in her friend's face, a sigh escaping her. 'Loveday, I can't explain, but it . . . it isn't like that. Please don't be so angry! I wasn't trying to steal him from you. I . . . I just don't know what to say——'

'Try the truth!' snapped Loveday.

Annis put her hands over her face, her shoulders shaking, a muffled sob breaking out of her. She was on the verge of telling Loveday the whole truth—it would have been a relief to her to tell someone—yet she still couldn't bear to talk about it. She couldn't face the questions, the way Loveday might look at her.

There was a silence, then Loveday moved closer, put a hand under Annis's chin and lifted her head firmly. Annis kept her eyes shut, but she felt Loveday inspecting her face, her puffy eyes, the track of tears down her cheeks. She pulled away, ran a trembling hand over her wet lashes and sniffed, hunting for a handkerchief in her bag. Loveday produced a pink tissue from the box of them on the powder-room wall.

'Here!' she said roughly.

Annis dried her eyes, then blew her nose. In the mirror, her pink-rimmed eyes met those of Loveday, who grimaced wryly at her.

'Sorry I snarled! You can't help it if you've fallen for him, too, I suppose! He bowls us all over without even trying—Mr Sex Appeal!' She laughed crossly, then sat down in the chair next to Annis and stared at herself in the mirror, her hazel eyes inspecting her red hair, her oval face, her figure, without enthusiasm. 'And I haven't got a chance with him, anyway. He's not really interested in me, he has always been more interested in you—don't think I didn't notice that! Why do you think I was always checking on how you felt about him? I'd seen the way he keeps looking at you.'

Annis looked down, her skin burning. Loveday watched her, and laughed shortly.

'Oh, I'm not stupid or short-sighted, don't worry! But you said you weren't interested, and I could tell you were trying to stay out of his way, so I hoped . . . Well, never mind! It isn't your fault, it's just typical of the way my life works out!' She gestured to the mirror. 'You'd better do something about your face before we go back, hadn't you?' she said in a more friendly voice, and Annis nodded.

She splashed lukewarm water on her face to reduce the puffiness, washed carefully, patted her skin dry, and began applying a little light foundation, then powdered over that, before she smoothed eyeshadow into her lids and put on lipstick, while Loveday watched her.

'Oh, well, plenty more fish in the sea!' she thought aloud in a wry voice, and Annis laughed.

'He's not so much a fish as a ship passing in the night, though,' she pointed out. 'Neither of us are likely to see him again. After all, we're leaving Corinth tomorrow.'

'That's true!' Loveday nodded. 'He's not worth quarrelling over. Sorry, Annis.'

Annis smiled at her in the mirror. 'Forget it. How do I look now? Back to normal?'

'Terrific,' said Loveday, and they went back together to find Raphael sitting at the piano while the hotel manager stood beside him, turning over a pile of sheet music.

'Oh, I'd forgotten he was going to play,' said Loveday. 'He asked you to turn over his music for him, didn't he?'

'He won't need me, he was kidding. He won't use a score—he memorises whole concertos.'

Loveday looked oddly at her. 'How do you know that?'

Annis flushed. Another little slip! Averting her eyes, she shrugged. 'I must have read it somewhere.'

As they walked to their table Raphael shot them a glance and beckoned commandingly to Annis. Loveday gave her a grin. 'What were you saying about him not needing you?'

Annis saw the hotel manager looking towards her, and realised that she wasn't going to be able to ignore Raphael, so she reluctantly walked over to the piano.

'I'm going to play this,' Raphael told her, taking a book of sheet music from the hotel manager's hand.

'My favourite piece of music!' the manager said, looking very pleased.

Annis glanced at the composer's name on the cover, and didn't recognise it.

'A brilliant modern Greek composer,' Raphael said, watching her.

The hotel manager smiled agreement.

'Do you know the piece?' asked Annis uncertainly, knowing that although he could sight-read he preferred time to study a piece before playing it in public, but Raphael nodded.

'It was written for a film, three years ago, and I conducted.'

The hotel manager bowed to him. 'May I announce you now, then, Maestro?'

Raphael looked amused at the reverential title, but nodded. 'I'm ready.'

The hotel manager went over to the band, who were playing while guests danced, and Raphael glanced up at Annis.

'Are you OK?' he asked tersely and she started, giving him a quick, uncertain look.

'Why?'

'You look washed-out.' His tone was brusque, but his eyes were concerned. 'You know this heat isn't good for you—what on earth prompted you to visit Greece in summer? You should have come in the spring.'

'It was the only time we could all get away from the office.'

'Oh, yes, this office—are you this Carl Worth's secretary?'

'Yes.' Her voice was flat, her face wary.

'So you're with him all day, in the same office?' Raphael bit out.

'Yes,' she admitted tensely, and then, with enormous relief, she heard the band stop playing. The hotel manager tested the microphone, coughed to clear his throat, and began a careful introduction in his excellent English.

The guests who had been dancing drifted back to their seats, clapping, and Raphael shifted on the piano stool, flexing his long, powerful fingers. 'Ready?' he asked Annis, his eyes fixed on the first page of the music, and she murmured agreement.

When the applause died away, Raphael began to play the gentle, elegiac music and Annis stood close to him, deftly turning the pages while she listened.

She had learnt to read music when she was having piano lessons as a child. She had not been particularly talented and had given up her lessons during her late teens, but she had not forgotten how to read music and still enjoyed playing a little from time to time, and her enjoyment had developed into a passion for listening to other people make music. She had given up her music when she'd realised she would never be very good, but she had still been sufficiently fascinated by music-making to want to work in the music business, which was how she had met Raphael.

She had been working as a secretary for a Manchester-based orchestra when Raphael had begun making regular appearances with them as guest conductor. He had been too busy with the other aspects of his career, with concerts abroad as a solo artist with other orchestras, with writing and conducting film music, and not least with recording, to want to work with them full time, but their regular conductor had been a very old man, and had found the concert schedule exhausting. In order to allow him frequent rest periods, the orchestra had begun having guest conductors from time to time, of whom Raphael was undoubtedly the most popular.

Raphael's mother had been English, the only daughter of a Manchester family who had founded a department store at around the turn of the century and had lived ever since in a large Victorian house, in a square with an old garden at its centre, in one of the most sought-after residential areas in the city. When his maternal grandfather died, Raphael had inherited the house and always lived there when he was in Manchester, but he had split the house into two flats. He kept the top floor for himself, but his sister, her husband and their two children lived in the other half of the house. Annis had been nervous of meeting Raphael's sister, Carmel, but to her relief they had got on like a house on fire from the very first.

They had often spent a family evening together—dinner, cards, talk, usually ending with Raphael's playing the piano for them. Carmel had learnt to play the flute as a child, but, like Annis, she had given up. 'I soon realised I could never be as good as Raphael,' she once wryly confided to Annis. 'And I wasn't going to be second-best! So I took up embroidery instead!'

Annis had wondered for a second if Carmel was jealous of her brother's fame and genius, but there was neither jealousy nor resentment between Raphael and his sister; they were much too close for that. Carmel had been born when Raphael was twelve years old. Until then he had been an only child, and her arrival had delighted him; he had always wanted a sister or brother, and was fascinated by the baby. Annis was to feel, as she had got to know them both better, that Raphael was a second father to his little sister, since their own father had died when Carmel was four, leaving the teenage Raphael as the man of the family. Carmel had married young. Her husband, Barry, was a car salesman; he had charm and good looks, but he was a weak man and given to extravagance, so that they rarely had much money, which was why they lived rent-free in a flat in Raphael's house.

A burst of clapping made Annis start; she turned dazed eyes on Raphael as he got up and bowed to the applauding audience of hotel guests. Annis had forgotten where they were and her face must have betrayed as much.

Raphael shot her a sideways look, his brows rising. 'Something on your mind?' The tone was mocking, and so were his grey eyes as he watched the slow flush creep up to her hairline. She was off balance enough to blurt out the truth.

'I was thinking about Carmel. How is she?'

His face iced up. 'I wondered if you would ever ask.'

She flinched at the bite in his voice. She deserved that; she should have asked after Carmel and her family the minute they met again, but her nerve had failed her. The audience were still applauding, and Raphael bowed towards them again, his smile tight.

'She isn't at all well,' he said tersely to Annis out of the corner of his mouth.

Annis murmured an incoherent regret. 'Oh, dear...I'm s——'

'Don't say sorry again! You never mean it!' he snapped, and she bit her lip, her flush dying and pallor taking its place.

'I do! I'm very fond of Carmel.'

'So fond that you've never been near her since you walked out on me?' he sneered, and she felt tears prick her eyes.

'That was...how could I? She was your sister and I knew how she would feel, but I was still fond of her.'

She got a black, glittering look at that. 'How nice! You were still fond of Carmel, but you didn't visit her because you couldn't stand the idea of running into me again?'

She didn't answer. He turned away from the still applauding audience and tidied the music on the piano in a rather automatic fashion, his face taut.

Roughly, he said, 'She never complains, that isn't Carmel's way...'

'No,' she agreed gently, watching his profile and aching for the pain she saw in his face. Raphael was staring blindly at the music sheets.

'But some days I can't bear to look at her, she's so frail and——' He broke off as the hotel manager came up, smiling and extending a hand.

'Wonderful! You have given us so much pleasure, thank you, thank you. Our guests are eager for you to play for us again—won't you, please? A little encore? We don't want to make you work too hard on your holiday, but——'

'Some other time,' Raphael said in a flat voice. 'I'm sorry, I'm too tired tonight.' He bowed towards the audience, who broke out in clapping again, but he didn't speak to them; he turned and took Annis by the elbow and walked away with her, out of the room, into the warm, moonlit night.

Annis dared not struggle while everyone watched them, but once they were outside in the hotel gardens she pulled away and stood still, her head up but her eyes fixed on the night sky rather than on Raphael.

'I think I'll go to my room now—it is rather late.'

'Not yet,' he said thickly. 'There's something I want to know—did you leave me because of Carmel?'

She stiffened. 'What?'

'You heard me! Is that why you backed out of marrying me? Barry thought that might be it. He said he thought you left because you were afraid you would be landed with looking after Carmel while I was away on tour.'

Annis felt rage flare inside her, burning her throat. Barry had accused her of that? Her hands screwed into fists at her side. 'And is that what you think of me?

That I'd turn my back on a sick girl? I was always happy to do what I could for Carmel. That had nothing to do with my leaving. It was...' She paused, swallowing, pulling herself up. She had decided in cold blood two years ago never to tell him, and however angry she might be she wasn't going to say something she would only regret.

'I told you why I was leaving,' she said quietly, 'I don't want to talk about it any more.' She swivelled to walk back into the hotel, but Raphael caught hold of her shoulder and pulled her round again to face him.

'Well, I do want to talk about it! Your letter said you'd met another man!' The grey eyes flashed over her face. 'Where is he?'

She was trembling. 'Please... just let me go, Raphael. Please.'

'Not yet,' he said, his mouth obstinate. 'I'm not letting you go out of my life again until I know the truth. Look at me, Annis. Look at me and tell me you're indifferent to me.'

She looked at him wildly and knew she couldn't lie then, not then, in this warm, sensual night with the moon showing her the strong, beautiful lines of his face, and those grey eyes fixed intently on her so that she had no hope of hiding her real feelings from him even if her tongue could frame a lie. She did the only thing she could do; the only thing she had done before when she fled from him.

She ran away, across the terrace, between the black shadows of trees and the silver pools of moonlight on the stone paths. Annis was so wrought up that she almost felt the air was heavy with foreboding; there was a strange stillness everywhere—even the cicadas were silent and the leaves on the trees did not so much as move. There was only a smouldering heat and the moonlight, and then a cloud passed over the moon and the night was very black.

Annis ran into the hotel and up the stairs, knowing that Raphael wasn't far behind her.

She reached her room and unlocked the door seconds before he caught up with her. She was inside in a flash, and would have slammed the door in his face if he hadn't thrown himself forward and crashed into the room almost at the same time.

'Go away, Raphael! Leave me alone!' she cried out in anguish.

His face was harsh. 'Is that what you really want?'

'More than ever,' she said, although it hurt unbearably to say it. It was true; ever since they had met again she had been wondering if there wasn't some way they could make it work for them, after all, but after what he had told her tonight she had known that in fact it was more impossible than it had been two years ago. There was no way she could go back to him.

'I don't believe you,' Raphael said hoarsely, reaching for her.

She fought like a wildcat, but he was stronger than her and dragged her close enough to kiss her, his mouth hot and angry. She struggled, pulling her head back, and that only made him violent; his mouth deepened the kiss, his hands were insistent on her, and Annis felt the room swim and waver around her. She shut her eyes, moaning, and the floor shook beneath her feet.

Raphael broke off the kiss. His head came up. 'What the hell was that?'

Annis stared at him dumbly, not understanding, and at that moment the world went crazy. There was a deafening rumble, the room collapsed inward and Raphael flung his arms around her as the floor went from under them and they began to fall.

CHAPTER FOUR

ANNIS woke up in darkness, feeling oddly stiff, as if she had slept in a cramped position all night. She thought at first that she was at home, in Croydon. It was very cold, and she shivered. Her covers must have slid off the bed, she must lean over and pull them up again, but just for the moment she somehow couldn't move. She must still be half asleep, she thought, yawning in a convulsive way. She would pick the covers up when she was properly awake.

It was so dark! She could not see anything. It was as if she had been struck blind. It must be the middle of the night, and yet she could hear the strangest sounds, muffled and distant; she couldn't make out what was being said, but somewhere people were shouting. She frowned. No, not shouting—crying and calling out. Or was she imagining it?

She didn't know why she felt so odd—was she ill? Was that it? Or... her mind suddenly leapt back in time to another dark, moonless night when she had been trapped and terrified, and her heart began to shake in her breast. She had been icy cold that night; she had trembled and been confused. She knew the symptoms of shock now. She had felt them then, and she felt them now. Was this a memory—or was it real? Was it a nightmare? She had used to have a recurring nightmare, night after night. Was she awake, or sleeping, and if she was awake who was screaming? People in the street? But at this time of night? Drunks? she thought. Foreign ones, too! She couldn't make out what they were shouting until she recognised a Greek word. Greek!

Everything came rushing back like flood waters over her head. She remembered the earthquake; she remembered falling. She remembered it all.

She gave a wild, involuntary cry of shock and pain. 'Raphael!' He had fallen with her—but where was he? Unconscious? Dead? Tears welled up in her eyes and rolled down her face. She must find him. She had to get out of here, get help, find Raphael. She tried to move, and gave a moan of pain, collapsing again. She couldn't. She could not move an inch. Pain was shooting through her; she began to realise she had been hurt, although she didn't know how—and she was pinned down by something heavy that lay across her midriff.

She put out a hand that shook, and felt a splinter run into her finger. Wood! She tentatively explored further, realising what it was—a wooden beam! She was trapped beneath a beam from a floor or ceiling. Maybe she could wriggle out from under it. She began a careful movement that ended abruptly with a grunt of agony. No. It hurt too much to move her leg.

She had to have help. She had to let people know she was here. She took a deep breath and began to shout. 'Help! Help!'

But after a few minutes she could hardly breathe and had to stop shouting. She lay there with a heaving chest, coughing and feeling sick. The air was full of dust, and had an acrid, smoky smell.

That was when the fear really began, as she worked out that she was buried under the rubble of the hotel in a pocket of air. The beam might have trapped her, but it had also saved her life because it was the beam that was shoring up the tons of rubble which might otherwise have crushed her. But what would happen when the air ran out?

She had begun taking frantic breaths, terrified of being unable to breathe at all, but suddenly she realised that the faster she breathed the sooner she would run out of air, so she forced herself to be calm. She had to stay cool-headed if she was to survive. She lay there very quietly for a moment, until her heartbeat had calmed down, and then she began to check herself for injury.

Her hands were bruised, grazed, scratched; she couldn't see that, but she felt it, and she realised, too, that the wetness trickling down from her forehead and cheekbone was blood. She tasted the salt of it in her mouth.

She could move her left leg freely, but a stab of pain went through her when she tried to move her right leg. Was it broken? Every movement was agonising. She knew, too, that she must have broken ribs because it hurt her even to breathe—but it could have been worse. It still could be worse. Her imagination went crazy. What if the building collapsed even further? What if she was crushed to death?

She began to hyperventilate again, dragging air into her lungs, panting; and again she made herself calm down, slow down, breathe slowly.

She must not think about death.

A sound made her stiffen, listening intently. It came again, a faint sound, barely audible. Breathing! she thought, with a leap of the heart. Someone was breathing nearby.

'Is someone there?' she whispered, then swallowed and tried again, in a stronger voice. 'Hello? Who's there?'

No reply. She turned her head that way and felt the rubble under her shift, so she lay still for a second, her eyes trying to pierce the darkness. She couldn't see anything at first, and then she began to see a shape, a solidity which was different from the gloom around it.

'Hello? Who is it? Hello!' she said, almost shouting. The silence made her shiver. Whoever it was could be too badly injured to be conscious, could be dying. She nerved herself, then stretched out her hand. In this darkness it was hard to judge the distance between herself and the other person; it seemed a long, long time before her fingertips touched something. Skin, she thought, tensing. Skin which was cold and damp with sweat. Her fingers delicately explored, traced the shape of cheekbones, eye sockets, a mouth, nostrils through which warm air was being breathed.

A deep sob shook Annis. She knew that face, even in the dark. She knew it as intimately as he knew her own, and she put her fingertips on his mouth, moaning his name.

'Raphael...darling...oh, my darling... Don't die...you can't, I couldn't bear it. Raphael, can't you hear me? Raphael...it's me...'

His lips moved faintly and her heart turned over as she realised he was kissing her fingers.

'Oh, Raphael, thank heavens...' she whispered huskily.

There was a silence, then she heard him shifting slightly, turning his head her way as if he, in his turn, was trying to pierce the darkness.

'Annis?' His voice was thready, weak. It made her stomach clench in fear—was he badly injured?

'Yes,' she answered and heard the sigh he gave.

'Are you in pain?' he asked with urgency, and she told him what she had worked out about her injuries.

'I've been lucky,' she ended with a wry humour.

'Lucky?' he repeated, half laughed, then coughed.

'Well, it could have been much worse!'

'Could it?' he whispered drily.

'What about you, Raphael? Still in one piece?' She was trying to keep the tone light, but she was terrified of what he might tell her.

'No idea yet,' he said, and she sensed that he was saving breath by saving on words. 'I...I suppose I'd better...' he took an audibly painful breath and finished '...find out the worst.'

She lay listening to his careful movements as he explored the extent of his injuries. Her nerves were stretched to breaking-point. He might be badly hurt. He might be dying. Oh, if only she could get to him, look after him! The waiting was like being stretched on the rack.

'Well,' Raphael said unsteadily, 'I think I've broken my legs, both of them.' Annis bit her lower lip to stop herself crying out. She heard Raphael breathing for a few seconds, then he went on in that shaky voice. 'Something's wrong with my shoulder, my chest hurts like the devil. I must have broken ribs. My face is bleeding—and I think I'm covered in bruises from head to foot, but otherwise I'm OK.'

She was weak with relief because it did not sound as bad as she had been dreading it would be. 'So, what's the good news?' she joked, and Raphael laughed faintly.

'I'm still breathing!'

She felt very odd then, and had to close her eyes while a wave of faintness passed over her. When she came out of it she heard Raphael urgently saying her name.

'I'm OK,' she said with an effort and heard him sigh.

'Did you pass out?'

'I felt faint, but it's gone now.'

They were both silent. They could hear the voices far away, and other sounds—the clatter and hum of engines, the crash of masonry. 'They've begun a rescue attempt, anyway,' Raphael said.

Annis suddenly gave a cry of shock. 'Oh, I'd completely forgotten Loveday and Carl... They were in the ballroom, the whole weight of the hotel must have fallen on them. What if—— ?'

'Stop it!' Raphael said harshly. 'Don't let your imagination run away with you. They probably got out safely. They were downstairs, remember, and there were Greeks with them, local people who may well have been through an earthquake before. They would have realised what was happening, and given the English guests a warning in time, whereas we were too busy to notice a little thing like an earthquake.' He began to laugh, and she was grateful for the darkness which hid her face from him. Raphael suddenly stopped laughing, a groan escaping him.

'What is it?' Annis asked anxiously, wishing she could see him.

'Nothing,' he said in a ragged voice, and she recognised the note of pain. She was in great pain herself.

'Are you cold?' she asked, her teeth chattering. 'I'm frozen. Isn't it odd? When you think how hot it was earlier today. The temperature must have dropped like a stone. If only we could move!'

'Just as well we can't,' said Raphael in a weary voice. 'We might start an avalanche of rubble.'

She shivered violently. 'Don't! How long do you think it will take them to...?'

'They'll get to us as fast as they safely can,' he said gently, his voice fading away in the distance. How odd, she thought. Surely she wasn't going deaf? Or was Raphael going to sleep?

Somewhere above them something crashed and the reverberations of the sound made her wake with a wild start. It was only then that she realised she had lost consciousness, and she called out, 'Raphael!' in blind terror.

'I'm here, darling!'

His voice was much clearer, firmer. She turned her head and suddenly she could make out a pale shape glimmering in the darkness.

'Raphael, I can see you!' she burst out and saw his mouth move. He was smiling.

'I can see you, too.'

'I must look terrible!'

He laughed, a weak, shaky sound, but laughter all the same. 'How like a woman! As if it mattered how you looked!' He was breathing audibly, as though it hurt. 'They must be using arc lights,' he added.

'Or it could be daylight,' Annis suggested. 'How long have we been here?'

'Who knows?'

Annis lay staring at where the light was filtering down to them. Not daylight, she thought. That was an artificial light.

'You're right,' she said. 'They're working by arc lights.'

Raphael didn't answer; she heard him breathing very faintly and fear almost stopped her heart.

'Don't die, Raphael!' she broke out but he didn't answer that, either. He was either asleep or unconscious, she realised, and lay very still, listening to him breathe. While he went on breathing, however lightly, he was alive, so she held on to consciousness herself to listen to him, as though that might keep him alive, but it was hard. She kept drifting in and out of a light doze.

The sounds above were getting stronger, coming closer. The mechanical sound of digging stopped and someone called out in Greek and then in English, and Annis cried out in English.

'Hello! We're here! Hello?'

The voice replied at once, 'How many of you are there?' and, when she had answered, asked about their injuries and promised that a doctor would get to them very soon to give them injections of a pain-killing drug. Then it was quiet again.

Five minutes later, Raphael woke up, shifted his position and gave a little grunt of pain because he had forgotten his injuries.

'We've had a visitor,' Annis said. 'And any minute now we should be getting another one—a doctor with a hypodermic needle!'

'I never thought I'd look forward to getting an injection,' Raphael muttered. 'I hate the things normally, but——' He broke off and Annis put her hand out to touch his cheek.

'I know. Pain is tiring, isn't it?'

'It hurts, too,' he said drily.

She smiled and at that instant they both heard the men working above them. Plaster crumbled down like fine creamy dust in the glare of the arc lights, and then a lump of concrete crashed down, missing them by inches, and Annis went stiff with fear.

'Be careful!' she burst out, and silence fell, then someone answered reassuringly and the digging commenced again. More and more light was coming through; they could see each other clearly and see movements high above them, blurs of colour from the clothes of the men digging. More rubble fell; some of it hit Annis and she gave a little cry of pain.

Raphael gave a roar of anger. 'Damn you! Be careful! Do you want to kill her?'

There was a round gap between the rubble now. A face showed through it, a man's eyes peering down at them. He didn't need to speak to tell them he was Greek—he had olive skin, black hair, black eyes—but although his accent was heavy he did speak a little English.

'We cannot get you out yet. Not safe. Too much...' He paused, frowning. 'Too much building on top of you? You are understanding me? But the mens will lower me to give you injections for the pain. Please to be patient. Not very much long now.'

The doctor disappeared again and a few moments later Annis watched as, in his white coat and safety helmet, he was lowered slowly, a rope around his waist. He knelt beside her and examined her, his face professionally blank, then put a safety helmet on her head. 'That will protect you if any more rubble falls on you,' he said, then asked, 'This is hurting you?' gesturing to the beam lying across her.

'No, it doesn't actually press down on me, and it's keeping all that rubble off me...but if it could be lifted I could move.'

'Not possible,' he said with a regretful smile. 'Not yet. But soon, I promise, when the workmen can get a machine into place to lift it. Let me give you something that will help, though. It will not hurt.' He produced a hypodermic needle from a sterile plastic box, carefully prepared her arm and injected her, strapped a dressing over the wound and then wrapped her in a blanket over which he lay a thin sheet of thermal foil before turning to examine Raphael. She knew at once that Raphael's injuries were far worse than her own. The doctor's tone changed. Annis felt her stomach clench in fear. She had guessed already that Raphael was more seriously hurt than he had told her—but just how bad were his injuries?

She listened with nerves stretched to the point of snapping while the doctor asked Raphael a series of questions to which he got only curt replies.

'Look, can I have that injection?' Raphael asked at last with a black impatience that told her just how much pain he was suffering. It was rare for him to be so harsh, but Annis had always been afraid of Raphael's occasional explosions of rage. That was why she hadn't dared tell him the real reason why she was leaving him. He would have blown too many lives sky-high.

The doctor made no comment on Raphael's bad temper; he gave him the injection at once, said soothingly that he was going to be fine, there was nothing to worry about.

Annis by then was floating on a sea of calm tranquillity as the warmth of the blanket and the outer foil covering percolated through her body and the drug took effect. The permanent grinding pain, which she had seemed to be suffering for hours, at last subsided. She sleepily repeated, 'Going to be fine, nothing to worry about.' It seemed a blissful thought, if she had been capable of thought, but her mind had stopped working.

The doctor had finished wrapping Raphael in a blanket and outer foil. 'How do you feel now?' he asked, and Raphael thanked him gruffly. 'Sorry to have been short-tempered,' he muttered.

'You were in pain. I understand,' said the doctor, closing his bag. 'You are both OK now? Good, good. Try to rest until we can get you out. I must go now. I have other patients waiting.' He gave a tug on the rope, and a face appeared in the small gap above. The doctor spoke in Greek, and the other man nodded.

Annis hurriedly said, 'Doctor, before you go... Some friends of mine were in the hotel too. Their name is Worth—Carl and Loveday Worth. Do you know if they are safe?'

'I am sorry,' the doctor said, smiling at her sympathetically. 'I cannot tell you anything. I am just looking after the injured. I do not know what is happening. But many English got out before the hotel collapsed. Most of the hotel guests are safe, I think, because they were close to the exits when the earthquake began. Very few people were trapped when the upper floors collapsed. You were unlucky!'

He was looking at them quizzically, and Annis flushed, realising that he must be speculating on the fact that they had been alone together in her bedroom when the earthquake happened. Only then did it dawn on her that it wasn't only the doctor who would be curious. Everyone would know, sooner or later, that Raphael had been with her! It was bound to cause a lot of talk. What on earth would Loveday think? Annis didn't look forward to facing Loveday when they were eventually rescued.

The doctor was tying the rope around his waist again. He smiled. 'But soon your ordeal will be over. We will get you both out in a very little time.'

'Thank you, Doctor,' she said, and he nodded before swinging slowly up on the rope to vanish from sight.

'Happy now?' Raphael drawled, and she looked round at him, faintly puzzled by the tone.

'I feel much better. I wonder what he put into us? Morphine? Does that make you feel laid-back and very relaxed?'

'I've no idea. Whatever the stuff was, it worked, but that wasn't what I meant. I was talking about Carl Worth. Have you been eaten up with worry over him all this time?'

She wasn't sure what he was getting at, but his tone made her uneasy. 'He's a friend...'

'Friend?' The question had ice on it and she frowned.

'Yes! And so is his sister! They've been very good friends of mine ever since I joined the agency.'

Raphael grunted, then asked, 'And how long ago was that?'

He was treading on dangerous ground again. 'Can we not talk about the past?' she muttered, and even that was a mistake because he came back at once, his tone needle-sharp.

'Why are you so scared of talking about the past? Which past worries you? The one you shared with me—or after that?'

'Oh, please! Not now!' The drug which had made her woozy and cheerful, as if she had had a few glasses of wine, did not seem to have had the same effect on Raphael. He was still on her trail, like some tenacious bloodhound, following the scent however difficult the territory.

'Why not?' he said aggressively. 'We have time enough, don't we? What else can we do? I know what I'd like to do with you, but while neither of us can move an inch that's out of the question...'

She coloured up at the implication of that, and he watched her sideways, his grey eyes sharp.

'We could play word games,' he mocked. 'You like word games, don't you? You're good at them, I remember, which made it all the more odd that you just wrote that letter before you bolted, and didn't talk to me face to face.'

He was trying to undermine her, but she was not going to let him taunt and torment her. She wasn't going to let him re-open that old wound—not again, not now. She didn't feel strong enough. The pain she had been in since they had crashed down through the collapsing hotel might have died down, but there was an older pain deep inside her which no drug could reach, and every word he said made it ache again. She felt weak and very, very weary. She knew she would never be able to argue with him. Raphael could always get the better of her in a verbal duel; his weapons were sharper. He might at times be gentle, but she had discovered now how cruel he could be, too.

She would have to distract him, but how? Only one idea occurred to her, so she said hurriedly, 'I'd rather hear some more about your last tour—it sounds great fun. What did you think of Turkey? You were in Istanbul, weren't you? Were the mosques fabulous? I've always wanted to see the Blue Mosque, it sounds so romantic, and the pictures I've seen of the interior are out of this world. I suppose you flew. Myself, I'd love to sail up the Bosporus at sunset and see the skyline with the sun setting behind it, all the mosques like black silhouettes against firelight.'

Raphael gave her an odd, crooked smile. 'Still a dreamer, Annis?'

'Yes,' she said defiantly.

His eyes were gentler suddenly. 'I did sail up the Bosporus on a ferry at sunset, and I did see the Istanbul skyline silhouetted against the setting sun, and it was wonderful.'

She smiled. 'Where else did you go on this tour?'

He tentatively shifted his position again. 'Paris,' he murmured, and her heartbeat quickened.

He waited for her to say something, but she couldn't get a word out, so Raphael said softly, 'For one night. Flew in, and out twenty-four hours later. I barely saw Paris. I stayed at that hotel we stayed at, remember?'

She remembered and a little sigh wrenched her.

'We had a marvellous week there, didn't we?' he said softly. 'Do you remember the concert on the Left Bank, and how we stayed up all night, ate supper, and then drank and talked with a bunch of students, and then walked over the bridges, looking into the Seine? We had our breakfast at a workman's café off the Boulevard Saint Michel, and I bought you red roses from a street-seller's basket, and put one behind your ear?'

She was trying not to remember, yet that made her smile. 'I must have looked pretty silly at that time of day, walking around Paris with a rose behind my ear.'

'Shall I tell you how you looked?' he asked, his voice husky, intimate, and her breathing grew audible.

'Don't start that again!' she said before she could call back the words, and Raphael looked at her with glittering, mocking eyes.

'What's the matter, Annis? You're breathing as if you've been on a marathon run!'

'Shut up!' she said, scarlet, and turned her head away to hide her face from him.

'Not that I could do anything about it,' he drawled. 'I can't move, so you needn't go into panic just yet. Save that for later, when I'm back on my feet and able to show you what you've been missing.'

She decided not to answer. In fact, she thought, it might be wiser to ignore him for a while, pretend to be asleep. The drug had made her very heavy, very drowsy, so it wouldn't be hard to fake sleep. She closed her eyes and concentrated on breathing in a regular way. Raphael was talking softly beside her, but she tried not to hear a word he said.

'You're a mystery, Annis, I don't understand you— or why you jilted me! And I'm not giving up until I know the answers to all my questions, so make up your mind. Sooner or later, you're going to tell me the truth about why you left and who you left with!'

She stayed silent, which wasn't hard because her pretence was almost a reality now as her tired mind gave way to sleep.

'Luckily for you, it will have to wait, though,' Raphael said. There was a long pause, then he said in a different voice, 'Annis? Are you OK?'

She only half heard him and it was easy to pretend she hadn't. After another pause, he sighed, and then Annis drifted away into total unconsciousness.

She woke up out of that recurring nightmare she had thought forgotten forever, and cried out in misery and fear, sweat running down her face, trembling violently.

'What is it, Annis?' Raphael's voice was tense with anxiety. The sound of it at first wove itself into her dream. She was torn with anguish between running to him and fleeing, the same old conflict, the dilemma from which she had run two years ago. 'Annis!' he said again, hoarsely, and then she broke free of the dream and woke up, remembering where she was and what had happened. Looking round, she saw his face far more clearly now. It was broad daylight.

'Have I been asleep for long?' she whispered shakily.

'Some hours,' he said. 'Why did you call out? Was it a nightmare? You were talking in your sleep...'

She was disturbed by that. 'What did I say?'

'I couldn't make it out. You said my sister's name once...' He was watching her when she turned her head; she saw his intent grey eyes fixed on her. 'If you didn't leave me because you couldn't cope with Carmel's illness, why should you be so upset about her? You sounded distraught just then. You were sobbing in your sleep.'

'I don't remember; it was just a bad dream,' Annis muttered. 'What time is it? My watch must have smashed when we fell—it isn't working.'

'Nearly seven,' Raphael said in a curt voice. He knew she had pointedly changed the subject and he didn't like it.

'Then we've been here all night?'

'All night,' he repeated drily. 'Just the two of us, alone, all night—and I couldn't move a muscle! What a waste of an opportunity.'

'Not alone,' Annis said. 'There are all those men out there, digging their way down to us.'

'How unromantic you are!' he mocked.

At that moment there was a noisy trickle of dust and brick, and the hole above them became a wide gap through which arc lights blazed, dazzling them. Annis saw grimy faces, under yellow safety helmets, white teeth showing in wide grins as the rescuers gave a spontaneous cheer at having broken through at last.

Minutes later, the beam was slowly raised and swung out of the way, and Annis was soon being lifted out into the daylight, her body wrapped in blankets and cradled by careful hands that passed her gently down to a waiting ambulance. She was conscious and could hear and see what was happening, and the injection she had been given was just wearing off so that she winced in pain despite the tender way she was being handled, but it was not her own condition that was worrying her. She could hear Raphael faintly, talking in English to the doctor who was supervising their removal from their night-long tomb.

'The only thing bothering me is my hands... They're covered in blood and one of them feels... well, numb, limp, it doesn't seem to move properly.'

The doctor murmured something soothing and Raphael exploded, his voice hoarse.

'Don't you understand? My hands are my life. I'm a pianist! I'll be finished if I can't use all my fingers.'

Annis whitened, closing her eyes. Oh, no! Not that! she thought. He hadn't breathed a word to her, it hadn't even entered her head that he was lying there fretting himself to death in case his hands had been maimed. Raphael's music had always meant more to him than anything else in the world. Whatever had happened to him, he had been able to seek comfort and refuge in his music, and when she'd left him she had been sure he would soon forget her in his private world of music. Music was essential to him. If Raphael couldn't play the piano he would wither inside.

CHAPTER FIVE

IT WAS not until the following day that she saw Loveday and Carl, and heard what had happened to them. Annis was in a private clinic in Athens by then. She knew that Raphael was there, too, but, like herself, he was forbidden to leave his bed. Some of the nurses spoke a little English, but they refused to discuss Raphael's condition, except to say that he was in no serious danger. Annis couldn't even get hold of an English paper to find out any of the details from the Press. She was not allowed to do anything at all for the first twenty-four hours. She was mostly asleep, anyway, of course, since she had been heavily sedated.

The following evening, though, Loveday and Carl arrived during visiting time, bringing her an armful of flowers.

She was listening to Raphael playing Rachmaninov on a tape, her headphones making her oblivious to everything else, and didn't notice for a moment as the door was pushed open, then her friends came into the room and her face lit up.

'Loveday! Carl!' She pulled the headphones off and dropped them on the bed, holding out her hands to her friends. 'I'm so relieved to see you! What happened to you? Did you get out of the hotel before the quake started? Are you OK?'

They looked perfectly normal, and they came to kiss her cheek and lay the flowers on the bed. Annis picked them up and breathed in their fragrance with pleasure.

'Thank you, they're lovely! I'll get the nurse to put them in water in a minute. Sit down, both of you, and tell me how you are.'

'How we are? Never mind us, look at you!' said Carl, running a sober eye over her strapped ribs and leg in plaster, the bruises and grazes visible on those parts of her left visible by her white cotton nightgown.

'Oh, it could have been worse. I'll live!' She had come too close to death to want to dwell on her injuries.

'Poor Annis!' said Carl, studying her face with shrewd eyes, as if he understood how she must feel. 'It must have been terrifying, and thank heavens it wasn't even worse.'

'That's what I've kept thinking,' she confessed, smiling at him. 'Even while we were trapped in the dark— and that was the really scary time, when they hadn't broken through yet and there didn't seem to be much air. I kept thinking we'd had it! But at least we were alive and we did have a chance of survival.'

Loveday shuddered. 'Don't talk about it any more! It scares me just to think about it.' She sat on the edge of the bed and contemplated Annis's face. 'You've got a black eye,' she informed her thoughtfully.

'I know I have!' Annis was not exactly delighted by the reminder. She had been staring at her bruised eye for a long time that afternoon and realising that it would be a long time before it healed. 'I'll have to wear dark glasses to hide it when I leave hospital,' she said grimly.

Loveday gave her a strange look. 'I suppose you didn't get it from Raphael?'

'Don't be ridiculous!'

'Well, I can't help wondering what the two of you were doing upstairs together!' Loveday's eyes were as sharp as knives.

Annis coloured angrily, and couldn't answer.

'Loveday! You said you weren't even going to mention that,' Carl said critically, frowning, and his sister made a face.

'Yes, well . . . if she had stayed with us she wouldn't be in this hospital now, would she?' Then Loveday looked at Annis again and groaned. 'Oh, I'm sorry, Annis. Take no notice of me, I'm just being a cat.'

'Old green eyes!' her brother said, and Loveday slapped him.

'And you can keep out of it! It's just between me and Annis, and we're much too smart to really quarrel over a man, aren't we, Annis?'

'Of course we are,' Annis said in relief because she had been dreading what Loveday would say when they met, and now the worst was over. 'You still haven't told me what happened to you during the earthquake.'

'Oh, we got out after the first little tremor,' Carl said calmly. 'The waiters rushed out, yelling, and we all got swept out with them into the gardens. We hadn't gone far before the hotel started making this awful rumbling, crashing noise and we looked round in time to see the whole place collapse like a pack of cards. We didn't realise you were inside until later, when our courier had a roll call and you didn't answer.'

'And then the hotel checked all the guests and found out Raphael was missing, too,' said Loveday in a very dry voice.

Annis changed the subject hurriedly before her friend could start quarrelling again. 'Has the coach party moved on to the seaside now?'

Carl nodded. 'The holiday is going ahead as planned, but the tour company made arrangements for us to visit you today. Paddy himself drove us. He's gone shopping, and he'll pick us up and take us back to our hotel after we've seen you.'

'That was thoughtful of him. Is the new hotel OK? Give my love to everyone else in the group. Are they enjoying the beach life?'

'They're worried about you, and send their love, but yes—they're all relaxing after that pretty strenuous tour.'

Annis had noticed an English newspaper in Loveday's straw beach bag. 'Could I see the paper?' she asked. 'The hospital doesn't seem to have any.'

'Keep it,' Loveday said casually dropping it on her bed. 'Have you let your mother know you're OK?'

'Yes, they let me telephone her this morning. She wanted to fly out here, but I told her I'd be home next week. They said I should be able to leave then. I'm not really ill and I should heal quite quickly. Of course, I'll still be bandaged up like an Egyptian mummy, but the airport will provide a wheelchair to and from the plane.'

'How long before you can come back to work?' asked Carl, adding hastily, 'Not that I'm pressuring you! We can manage without you, although we'll miss you, of course.'

'I don't know yet, but it shouldn't be long. I suppose it will be once I've had the plaster on my leg removed. It might be a bit awkward hopping on and off Tube trains, although it would come in handy as a lethal weapon if anyone tried to mug me!'

They talked cheerfully until the end of visiting time, when Carl said, 'We won't be able to come again, I'm afraid—until we return to Athens to fly home. But we'll keep in touch with the hospital to make sure you're OK, and we'll see you back home in London. Look after yourself.' He bent and kissed her. Annis would have turned her cheek, but he was too quick for her and managed to kiss her mouth.

Annis went pink, but Carl was already moving to the door. Loveday gave her a kiss on the cheek and then she

was gone, too, and Annis lay back against her pillows,
feeling lonely. They had written their names in fibre-
tipped pen on her plaster cast. She stared at the signa-
tures, her mouth crooked. Lying in this room without
anyone to talk to hour after hour was making her feel
very depressed.

She sighed and picked up the newspaper Loveday had
given her, wondering if there would be anything about
the Greek earthquake in it. She found it on the foreign
pages inside—it caught her eye at once. A large photograph of Raphael and a headline with his name promi-
nent in it. 'Famous Composer Buried Alive.' Beneath
that a smaller headline expanded the theme. 'Greek
earthquake hotel collapses.'

Annis read the copy hurriedly to find out if there was
recent news of Raphael, but the journalist knew no more
than herself. Raphael was seriously injured and recovering in a private clinic in Athens, she read. The re-
porter mentioned rumours that there were injuries to his
hands, but clearly had been unable to get confirmation
of the rumours. For Annis the mere mention of the
possibility was proof enough that there was fire behind
the smoke. She remembered hearing Raphael talking
grimly about his hands, and if the Press had picked up
the fact Raphael must have been right, his hands must
have been hurt.

But how badly? And could anything be done about
it? Annis stared at the photograph, tears glistening in
her eyes. It had been taken at a concert: Raphael in
evening dress, a baton in his hand, standing on a rostrum
with an orchestra in the background. He was not smiling.
She knew that look—Raphael was about to conduct; he
was tense, wrought-up, on edge, and it showed. That
was the sort of man he was—intense and fully com-
mitted. In his music, as in his life. All or nothing, that

was Raphael, and if he could not play the piano it would wound him deeply.

Of course, he would still have a life in music. He would no doubt go on composing, and as long as he was fit enough he would still be able to conduct, but that would not compensate Raphael for the loss of his ability to make music on a piano. Nothing would ever make up for that.

She asked next day if she could be wheeled in to visit Raphael, but it was not until she had been in hospital for four days that a nurse finally helped her into a wheelchair and pushed her along the corridor to Raphael's room. Her heart began to beat violently as they reached the door.

It wasn't going to be easy to say goodbye to him again. This time, in fact, it would be harder, because she had been through a parting once, and she knew now how lonely she was going to be.

Raphael lay surrounded by vases full of flowers, no doubt from his many fans all over Europe. He watched the nurse wheel her over to his bedside, his grey eyes unreadable. Annis tried to smile, but her mouth merely quivered.

'Hello,' she said shyly, very aware of the nurse listening to her.

The nurse said in husky English, 'I come back.' She held up both hands. 'That long.'

'Ten minutes,' Raphael drily translated as the young woman vanished through the door. He was staring, eyes narrowed, and Annis put a hand up in front of her face, very self-conscious.

'I know, I've got a black eye, but it's fading. Don't stare. How are you?'

'How do I look?'

She tried to smile again, but her mouth wouldn't obey her. Raphael looked heart-rendingly weak; he was pale and had even more bruises and cuts on his face than she had. His hair had been shaved away on one side of his head so that the doctor could get to an injury, his chest was strapped up, he had an arm and both legs in plaster, but it was at his hands that Annis had first glanced, her heart sinking. They were both bandaged.

Raphael had watched her with those impassive eyes. 'That bad?' he said, mouth sardonic.

She felt like crying, but she fought back the tears and answered, 'Oh, you look great!'

'Liar!' he said, and smiled with sudden tenderness, making her heart turn over.

She looked down, flushing, then asked nervously, 'Have you had any other visitors?' She didn't know how she could cope if someone walked into the room while she was there.

He shook his head. 'I've been sedated most of the time. Carmel can't get here, of course, but we talked on the phone. Barry offered to fly over, but I didn't want him to leave Carmel and the kids.'

'No, of course,' Annis murmured raggedly, and Raphael gave her a narrow-eyed stare.

'What about you? I suppose Carl Worth has been to see you?'

She pretended not to hear that. She was looking at the massed flowers. 'I expect your friends are queuing up to see you, though.'

'I've asked them all to wait until I'm up to talking.'

'If you aren't feeling up to talking, maybe I should go,' she said uncertainly, and he grimaced.

'If I hadn't wanted to see you, you wouldn't be here!'

'No, I suppose not,' she accepted, her mouth crooked. She could just imagine the nurses trying to persuade

Raphael to see someone he did not want to see! Her gaze wandered aside to headphones lying on a chair. 'At least you can listen to music.'

He gave her that sardonic smile. 'Don't ask me to count my blessings, please! Yes, I can still hear music and going deaf would be the ultimate agony, but I'm not in a very saintly frame of mind.'

'Beethoven survived going deaf.'

'I'm not Beethoven!'

She surveyed him, her head on one side. 'You look almost as morose!'

He grimaced. 'Thanks.'

Her gaze was drawn to his hands again, though she fought against it. 'Your hands,' she whispered. 'How serious . . . ?'

'They don't know yet.' His voice was curt. 'They had to operate and they aren't sure if it was successful.'

She bit her lip. 'I hope it has worked,' she said huskily, and he nodded.

'Thanks.' He was angry that she had even mentioned it, she saw that. He was trying not to think about it. 'They tell me you can go home in a week.'

'With any luck, yes.'

'Don't.' The word was brusque, and made her start, blue eyes wide. 'Stay until I go,' Raphael added in the same tone.

She didn't have to answer. The nurse reappeared, smiled at them both and said, 'Time now for goodbyes.'

Annis leaned forward and put her hand over one of his bandaged ones. 'I'm sure your hands are going to be OK,' she said hurriedly.

He just said, 'Come again tomorrow.'

She knew she shouldn't see him again, but she couldn't refuse. He made her heart ache.

Over the following week she visited him for longer and longer periods. They talked, listened to music together, she read to him. He couldn't read easily because of his bandaged hands, and as he only spoke a little Greek watching the local television was hard, but he had a pile of books on his bedside locker and Annis read her way through a great many of them with him. He always asked if Carl and Loveday had been to see her again, and when she said that it was too far for them to come, and, after all, they were on holiday, Raphael mocked, 'A rather lacklustre love-affair!'

'I told you!' she said impatiently. 'We're just friends!'

'Do you confide in him?'

She looked blankly at him. 'How do you mean?'

'Have you told him about the guy you left me for?'

Annis felt like screaming. He nagged away at her as if she were a sore tooth. 'No!' she snapped. 'Can we change the subject?'

'Fine,' he drawled, letting those grey eyes wander all over her, and she felt heat rise in her face, reminded that she was only wearing her cotton nightgown and over that a long, pale blue cotton robe. 'What a sexy dressing-gown!' Raphael teased, and that made her laugh, because she knew it was no such thing.

'I lost everything I had with me when the hotel collapsed, and had to wear hospital nightgowns until Loveday brought me these. She didn't know if I'd want to wear something glamorous or something practical, so...'

'She chose something practical?'

'Well, cotton is sensible in this climate. Nylon sticks to you, and silk is too expensive, anyway.'

'I'm wearing silk pyjamas,' Raphael said.

'You can afford to!'

'And they don't cling—feel!' he invited, and laughed mockingly when she flushed. Annis was relieved when the nurse appeared to help her back to her own room. She no longer needed a wheelchair; she was encouraged to walk about a little, with the help of a stick, but she was supposed to have a nurse with her to make sure she didn't run into any problems whenever she left her room.

Loveday and Carl came to see her the morning of the day they were leaving Greece. 'I wish we didn't have to leave you,' Carl said uneasily. 'Couldn't they transfer you to a hospital in London?'

'Any day now, I think. I'm much better,' she said, and Carl smiled.

'You certainly look it. There's been an enormous change since the last time we came! Well, get back home as soon as you can, won't you? We'll miss you badly.'

She asked her doctor when she could fly back to London the following day, and he said she could go as soon as she had made the necessary arrangements. When she told Raphael that she was leaving, he asked her not to go yet. 'An old friend who has a villa on a Greek island has offered it to me while I'm recovering——' he began, and she interrupted.

'I know what you're going to say and I can't do it,' she said huskily. The very idea of being alone with him for weeks made her panic.

'You might think about it! Look at my hands! What are you afraid of? What the hell do you think I'm going to do like this? I can't walk or swim. I can't play the piano. I can't even read a book. What am I supposed to do all those weeks while I'm convalescing? Lie in the sun like something cooking? That isn't even safe any more. Listen to music alone hour after hour? I'll go crazy, Annis!'

She heard the panic, the fear and anger in his voice, and felt desperately sorry for him. She would give anything to stay, look after him, make these anxious weeks pass peacefully for him, but how could she risk it? What if he had visitors? She was afraid of being forced into an intolerable position.

'There must be someone else who would come,' she murmured uncertainly.

'I don't want anyone else,' he said obstinately, his jawline rigid with determination.

Her heart leapt, but she looked away, turning pale with misery. She must not weaken—she dared not.

'You have so many friends,' she whispered.

'Look,' he ground out with harsh impatience, 'the next few weeks are going to be pretty tense, while I wait to find out if I'll ever play again, and I need peace and quiet. I don't want friends tiptoing about being tactful. I don't want people who can swim and go for walks while I just have to lie there like a log! And the very last thing I need is some woman trying to be sexy and exciting every time I set eyes on her! You need to convalesce, too. You won't be able to walk far or swim. We both love the same music and you enjoy reading aloud, you always have. A holiday in the sun would be ideal for both of us!'

She bit her lip, searching for some way of saying no that wouldn't make him even angrier, but then her eyes met his and Raphael's grey eyes pleaded, the need and fear visible in them.

'Please, Annis,' he said in that low, husky voice. 'Do I have to beg?'

How could she refuse?

They could not leave hospital until the specialist felt Raphael was fit enough to travel, and so it was another ten days before they flew to the little island, in a private jet owned by the friend who had lent Raphael the villa. Raphael had omitted to mention that his benefactor was a Greek shipping tycoon, but Annis realised as much when she saw the name painted on the side of the jet as they boarded. She had once met Silvio Diandros, a great music lover, when he had come back stage to congratulate Raphael after a concert in London.

Raphael was carried aboard on a stretcher; Annis boarded normally, leaning on her stick. They were the only passengers on the luxuriously furnished plane, and were served with champagne and caviare during the flight, which only took half an hour. From the window Annis watched the deep blue, sparkling sea below them as they circled before coming in to land on the mountainous island which looked quite unreal to her from the air—like a map in an atlas. Green valleys, grey rocks, brown and purple moorland lay flattened below the plane.

When they landed, their jet was met on the tiny airfield by a uniformed nurse and a local doctor, who came aboard to check on Raphael and Annis before they were satisfied that they could be taken down to an ambulance, which was parked right next to the plane so that they could easily be transferred from one to the other. Even so, Annis anxiously noted Raphael's pallor as they drove away. He had his eyes closed and she saw sweat pearl his forehead as the ambulance jolted over the grass. He must feel every little bump.

'Is it a long drive?' she asked the nurse, who was sitting in the back of the ambulance with them.

'Only ten minutes, but the roads here are very rough, so I'm afraid it will not be a comfortable drive.' The nurse was Greek, with dark eyes and dark hair, but she spoke flawless English. The doctor had already left, but the nurse was to stay in the villa in case either Raphael or Annis needed help. She had told them her name, but

Annis could not remember it, only that it was rather long and unfamiliar.

'Do many people live on this island?' Annis asked and the other woman shook her head.

'Around five thousand altogether, I think.' Her voice was kept low, very soft. 'There is a small town four miles that way.' She gestured back to the airfield. 'Dr Spiriatou practises there. There is a population of a thousand or so. Then there are a few villages along the coast, fishing villages which also have some tourists in the season. And inland there are some smaller villages, up in the mountains, far more isolated. The people there grow grapes and olives, run goats and sell cheese and milk, keep a few hens—scratch a living as best they can.'

'You've always lived here? Your English is very good.'

'Thank you.' The black head inclined gracefully in recognition of the compliment. 'I grew up here, and I learnt some English at school, but then my father died, and my mother took me to England to live with my sister, who had married an English journalist. I went to school there for a year, then I started training as a nurse in a hospital in Manchester.'

'Manchester?' Annis's blue eyes opened wide and she stared back at the other woman in astonishment. 'But that's where I come from!'

'Do you? That is a coincidence! Where did you live?'

Annis told her, and they talked for some time about the city they both knew so well, then Annis said, 'Nurse Mal...Malnxth...I'm so sorry, I can't pronounce your name...' Annis was flushed, embarrassed, but the nurse smiled with obvious amusement and no surprise.

'Please, call me Melina. It is easier.'

'I'm Annis. Tell me, Melina, are you working for Raphael, or this Greek tycoon who owns the villa?'

'I was sent here by Mr Diandros. He knew I came from here originally. I work for his company in Athens; he has his headquarters there and I am one of a team of nurses working for the shipping line. We take it in turns to staff the cruise liners or work in the office building in Athens, and if he wants a private job done for his own family one of us does that, too.'

'It was very thoughtful of him to send you here to look after Mr Leon.'

Melina gave her an odd look. 'Oh, I was here already. He rang and told me Mr Leon was coming and asked me to meet the plane with Dr Spiriatou.'

'Oh, you're on holiday here?' Annis conjectured uncertainly, and Melina shook her head.

'I was here looking after Diona Munthe.'

'The singer? I read somewhere that she had been taken ill. Does she live here?'

'She has been staying in Mr Diandros's villa for a month.'

This news was a shock and Annis glanced hurriedly at Raphael—did he know the famous singer was staying here too? Or had Diandros forgotten to tell him that? Annis had seen Diona Munthe sing several times. Very beautiful, Diona was in her early thirties. She had long black hair, a sensual figure and, surprisingly, green eyes, which must be inherited from her American-German father, who had married a Greek girl who came over to work for him as a housekeeper. Diona Munthe had become one of the most popular singers of the decade when she'd made her début in the lead role of Bizet's opera, *Carmen*, several years ago. Since then she had sung all over the world.

'Is she still here?' she asked with some apprehension because, although she had never met Diona Munthe, she knew her reputation as a somewhat arrogant, de-

manding woman, and the idea of sharing a villa with
her was not a very attractive prospect.

Melina looked amused, maybe guessing at Annis's reaction. 'For the moment, yes, but she is due to move
tomorrow to a small villa in the village nearby.' She
smiled at Annis wryly. 'This is not a rich island, but
even here things are changing. People from over there
have discovered us!' She flung out a hand as if pointing
to the mainland of Greece, hidden in the pearly sea mists
which veiled the horizon as dusk fell. 'From Athens,
mainly, you see—they came here on holiday and fell in
love with the island, so they started buying little houses
in the seaside villages, and they keep yachts here. They
come every weekend to sail and swim, but it has pushed
up the prices of houses, and of course it has meant that
more new houses have been built for them. Mr Diandros
has rented the little villa from the local agency for
Madame Munthe and her maid.'

'But you aren't going with them?'

'No, Madame Munthe is quite well now. She does not
need me, but when Mr Diandros heard that Raphael
Leon needed somewhere private and peaceful to convalesce he at once rang to offer both his villa and my
services.' Melina grinned with sudden impishness. 'At
this rate I will be here for the rest of my life! Mr Diandros
knows so many famous people, and they keep falling
ill!'

The ambulance swerved suddenly and slowed, then
came to a stop. 'The villa has electronically controlled
gates,' explained Melina as Annis looked enquiringly at
her. The ambulance began to move again a moment later,
and through its tiny windows Annis saw lawns and
around them cypress, pine and olive trees. Beyond that
she saw a dazzle of white walls, above them an ochre
roof. A columned terrace ran along the front of the villa,

deep with inviting bluish shade, and stone urns filled with brilliantly coloured flowers.

Raphael shifted, opening his eyes and giving a quick glance around the ambulance, looking faintly confused, as though not sure where he was. Annis smiled at him in instinctive reassurance. 'We've arrived at the villa,' she said gently.

His expression lightened. 'I'm amazingly tired,' he said, as if apologising.

'It was a long trip for you,' said Melina, and he stared at her as if he didn't remember ever seeing her before.

The ambulance parked right outside the front entrance of the house, and the driver and his assistant came round to lower the ramp at the back of the vehicle, then they lifted Raphael's stretcher down and carried him into the villa. Melina deftly helped Annis to manoeuvre her way down the ramp and across the terrace.

As they slowly made their way into the hallway, they heard a deep, honey-toned voice talking huskily. 'And when I heard that you were in Corinth when the quake hit, buried under the rubble, and perhaps dead, I wept, Maestro! This is too much, I said. This I cannot bear, for Leon to be dead! Such music to be silenced. This cannot be! And then the news came that you were found and you were alive but very ill, and Diandros rang and I said to him lend the Maestro the villa. "Please!" I said. "I am better now, I give up the villa to him."'

Annis halted in the doorway and watched Diona Munthe, on her knees beside the stretcher on which Raphael lay. There was something theatrical about her pose, her long, pale, swanlike neck submissively bent, the black hair wreathed on top of her head and pinned there with a *diamanté* comb. Delicately, Diona placed a kiss on Raphael's bandaged hand.

'Only get well, Maestro, that we may all hear your music once more!'

Annis was reminded of a scene in some opera, and was irritated by the look on Raphael's face. He was loving it. Well, of course he would, wouldn't he? A famous, not to say very beautiful and sexy woman kneeling in front of him, kissing his hand and calling him Maestro in throbbing tones? His ego must be purring like a cat after a saucer of cream.

'How generous, Diona,' he murmured, smiling. 'Just like you...kind and tender-hearted, always...'

Annis distinctly heard Melina sniff, and looked sideways. Melina met her eyes, her mouth derisive, impatient. She did not have a very high opinion of Diona Munthe either. Annis grinned at her, suddenly liking her very much.

The little sound had alerted Diona Munthe to their presence, however. She turned her head, green eyes narrowing. Raphael looked at them, too, his lids half down over his mocking eyes. Annis eyed him back, her mouth indenting. He need not think she cared if he flirted with the singer. If he had known that Diona was going to be here, perhaps he wouldn't have wanted her to come with him. Well, she could always leave, fly back to London. Her angry, defiant eyes told him as much, and Raphael considered her with a glittering threat in his smile.

'Who is this?' Diona asked, getting to her feet in a graceful movement. She did everything with grace, always aware of being watched and always centre-stage.

Raphael introduced them lazily. 'Annis was injured in the earthquake, too, and is here to convalesce.'

Annis smiled politely and put out a hand, but Diona ignored it.

'Diandros did not say you were bringing her!'

'Didn't he? He must have forgotten,' said Raphael, smiling.

Diona's catlike eyes held open hostility, her full mouth pouted sullenly.

Annis wasn't surprised; she had met too many singers not to know how they could react to any threat of competition. Raphael was both important and influential, and his fame was growing every year. Diona was at the top of her career, but she was shrewd enough to want to get to know him much better. For an ambitious singer it was always wise to get close to someone of Raphael's stature in their business. She must have jumped at the chance of spending time alone with him here, in such a romantic setting, especially when he was at a low ebb physically, and, she had no doubt calculated, vulnerable.

Had Diona been hoping to start a love-affair with him? He would, after all, make a very useful lover for a singer. Annis swallowed, hot with rage and jealousy as she realised that her own presence wouldn't necessarily stop Diona making a big play for him. Diona was too ruthless a player to back off because of another woman.

Well, I'm not staying here to play the third side of a triangle! she decided bitterly. She was leaving as soon as a flight could be arranged.

CHAPTER SIX

THE next day, Annis woke very early to a room full of blue shadows and pale, primrose light and a beautiful silence which she immediately registered since, at the hospital, she had woken every day to the busy sound of the daily routine. Cleaners, doctors, nurses, visitors—people trooped up and down the corridors, day and night. Doors slammed, telephones rang, vacuum machines and floor polishers hummed, voices and laughter came from all sides. She had got used to it, it had faded into the background, but now she noticed the absence of it as soon as she opened her eyes, and lay there uncertainly listening to the sound of silence.

Gradually, though, she picked up little sounds she had not heard at first: the murmur of the sea, apparently close by, dogs barking, hens cackling, a shutter being pushed open somewhere in the villa and something being shaken out of it. Annis lazily speculated on whether a rug or a continental quilt was being shaken, and then wondered with a yawn what time it was.

Leaning on her elbow, she picked up the clock and was surprised to see that it was nearly nine. She became conscience-stricken at once. They shouldn't have let her sleep. That was something else she had become accustomed to in the hospital. Waking up at crack of dawn!

Annis sat up carefully and swung her legs out of bed. Getting washed and dressed was a lengthy operation. She couldn't have a bath, because of her strapped ribs and the plaster cast on her leg, so she went through a slow process of washing herself from head to foot, and then got dressed. Her unpacking had been done for her last night while she ate her supper. She had very little with her, anyway, since all her possessions had been lost in the earthquake. The day before they had left Athens, Raphael had made arrangements for her to be driven into the city to a department store where she was able to buy a new wardrobe. He had insisted on paying for it and, as Annis had also lost her Greek money, along with everything else she had had with her, she had reluctantly allowed Raphael to lend her the money, although she was determined to pay him back as soon as she could. She had talked to her mother on the telephone before they had left Athens, and her mother was making arrangements to cable money through to her.

Annis hadn't been extravagant. She had bought the bare minimum of clothes: sandals, lingerie, a couple of swimsuits, several thin summer dresses, some shorts and tops and a pair of cotton trousers. Melina had sent up a young Greek girl called Irena who had put away all the clothes deftly while throwing fascinated glances at the girl in the bed. Annis had tried to thank her, but Irena knew little English, so Annis had communicated in sign-language, which had amused Irena into giggles.

If I were going to stay on, I'd learn some Greek while I was here, thought Annis, dropping one of her new dresses over her head and shivering. Cool, ice-blue cotton, it felt very good on her skin, but it wasn't the dress that made her shiver. It was the thought of going away.

She didn't want to leave—it made her feel sick to think of going and never seeing Raphael again—but the idea of watching Raphael and Diona Munthe flirting was even worse. Later this morning she would tell Raphael, ask him to arrange for her to fly back to Athens and then home to England, but for the moment she couldn't bear to think about it.

She opened the shutters on the window and her eyes were dazzled by the morning light. Pushing the window wide open, she leaned on the sill to breathe in the sweet air, her eyes half closed as she tried to identify the various elements in it. The scent of flowers, the salt of the sea, a faint, delicious smell of coffee.

A tap on the door made her turn, eyes startled. 'Come in!'

'Good morning!' It was Melina, in a crisp white uniform, not a hair out of place, smiling cheerfully.

'Good morning.' Annis smiled back. 'You shouldn't have let me sleep like that. I've wasted half the morning.'

'If you slept well, it was not wasted. I heard you open your shutters. Will you come down for breakfast on the terrace, or would you like it up here?'

'I'd much rather eat it on the terrace, thank you.'

'Do you need any help getting downstairs?'

'I think I can manage, but if you could be there to catch me?' Annis gave her a wry grin and Melina laughed.

'Of course.'

'Is Raphael awake?'

Melina nodded. 'He rang down for his breakfast an hour ago.' She watched Annis making her way across the room. 'You walk very well with that stick. You aren't in any pain? Good. Did I show you how to operate the house phone, if you want anything?'

'Yes, it just didn't occur to me to use it,' said Annis, smiling.

As they made their way down the wide corridor voices sounded in a room they were passing; Annis heard Raphael's deep tones, then a trill of laughter. She recognised Diona Munthe's voice at once, and stiffened.

So did Melina. 'She doesn't waste time!' she commented drily.

The two of them exchanged glances. Annis asked, 'When is she supposed to be leaving?'

'This morning, at eleven o'clock.'

'Unless she decides to stay.'

Melina shook her head. 'Mr Diandros has given orders for her to move out. She won't stay against his wishes. Her maid has already gone ahead with her luggage, to get the little villa ready for her, and the car will come back for Madame Munthe. But she won't be very far away, you know; I expect she will always be paying us a visit!'

'How nice,' Annis said with a hollow ring.

Irena served her coffee and rolls with thick, sweet black cherry jam on the sunlit terrace looking down over the gardens. The sun was climbing up the sky, but the black shadows of the pines and cypress still lay across the lawns, and water glistened on the grass and flowers where the gardener had been busy with his hose.

Melina had a cup of coffee with her, then got up, saying, 'Well, I must go and give Mr Leon his massage. He needs daily therapy sessions until he can move about normally. It's very easy for muscles to atrophy if they aren't used. I'll give you some massage, too, later this afternoon.'

'I wish I could swim,' Annis said rather mournfully, contemplating the blue water of the pool she could see through the trees.

'Pity, isn't it? Never mind, it won't be long now before you have your plaster cast removed.'

Annis spent the next hour on the terrace, glancing over some old American magazines without real interest, her mind lazily wandering.

She was just beginning to get bored when a car drove up and parked outside the house, and then Melina and Diona Munthe came out on to the terrace. Diona looked utterly stunning in a topaz silk trouser-suit which gave her skin a golden glow and made her eyes as brilliant as polished emerald. She paused to stare at Annis, those eyes narrowed and glittering.

'Ah, you!' she said slowly. 'I wanted to have words with you.' She looked at Melina, her face arrogant. 'I left my sun-hat upstairs—go and get it, will you?'

Melina looked furious, opened her mouth to argue, then fell silent under the singer's hard stare and went back into the house.

Diona Munthe leaned on the balustrade rail of the terrace and folded her arms, her beautiful body languidly posed. She had a magnetism Annis knew she couldn't match. They were very different types—Diona had fire and an almost blatant sexuality; Annis was very English, very understated, her blonde hair and blue eyes icy cool. Watching the other woman made Annis feel dull and unattractive.

'Mr Leon has told me why he brought you here,' Diona said with contempt. 'He felt he had to, because you were buried under that hotel with him. No doubt you think you've been very clever, making him feel responsible for you, just because you're far away from home and have lost all your luggage and money.'

'I didn't ask him to feel responsible for me!' Annis burst out furiously, and Diona gave her a chill smile.

'Don't try to lie to me. I know how easy it can be to twist a man around your finger. They can be such fools. But your little game is over now. I don't want you around, you would get in my way. I'll make a deal with you. I know you've had a rough time lately, so I'll pay for you to have a holiday in a good hotel for a week, and then I'll pay your fare home, first-class!'

Annis stared incredulously. 'Do you really expect me to accept?'

Melina came out of the house and walked towards them.

'It's a generous offer,' Diona said in a lowered, hurried voice. 'Think it over. I'll be here for lunch tomorrow. Give me your answer then.'

She turned away and took the hat Melina held out to her. Annis stood there burning with angry humiliation while the other woman swayed her way down the steps and climbed into the car.

'What was she saying to you?' asked Melina curiously.

'She was being insulting!' muttered Annis.

'She usually is. Take no notice!'

Annis moved slowly towards the house, leaning on her stick, wishing with even more fervour than usual that she could run. Her head buzzed with all the things she was going to say to Raphael when she got to his room. How dared he give that woman the impression that she had forced him to bring her here? Well, she was going to tell him exactly what she thought of him, and then she was going to demand to be flown back to Athens and home to England. She wasn't staying here another day. She wouldn't stay another hour if she could think of somewhere else to go. Maybe there was a hotel on the island. Hadn't Melina said something about a hotel in that little town she had pointed out at the airfield? Perhaps they might have a free room?

She reached Raphael's door almost breathless, and leaned on her stick for a moment to get her breath back before she flung the door open and faced him.

He wasn't in bed, as she had expected. He was reading a book, leaning back in a wheelchair by an open french window which led out on to a balcony. His black head lifted, he glanced sideways, and his mouth curved in a gleaming, inviting smile.

'I was wondering when you would come,' he murmured huskily, and to her fury she felt her stupid heart skip a beat. She wasn't going to let him hoodwink her like that, though. She moved doggedly forward, closed the door behind her with a little slam and stared belligerently at him.

'How dare you tell that woman such lies?' she burst out. 'Giving the impression that I made you bring me with you. Practically accusing me of blackmailing you. It wasn't my idea, it was yours. I wanted to go home, you know very well I did. I won't have you telling Diona Munthe lies about me——'

'I didn't tell Diona anything about you,' he bit out impatiently, but she shouted over him.

'Don't interrupt me! I haven't finished. You begged me to come to the island, you said you were going to be bored stiff all on your own. But that was before you found out she was here, wasn't it? Now you don't need me any more, so you're trying to think of a way of getting rid of me, and Diona was happy to do the dirty work for you. She told me what you said—that you had had to ask me because you felt responsible for me. Well, you needn't feel responsible any more, if you ever did. I'm perfectly capable of looking after myself. I'll go to a hotel on the island until I can fly back to Athens and on to London.'

'The hotel is fully booked!' he snapped.

'How do you know that?' she asked suspiciously, her face burning and a jealous ache deep inside her. 'Have you tried to book me in there already and been told there were no rooms?'

'No, I haven't, and I'm not going to,' Raphael said through his teeth, glowering. 'But Diandros tried to book Diona and her maid into the hotel, when he offered me this place, and every room was occupied. They have some tie-in with a holiday company who book all their rooms for the whole season. That's why he had to put her into a holiday villa.'

Annis thought frantically. 'Well, when can I fly back to Athens?'

'You're staying here!' Raphael said tersely, his grey eyes the colour of the sea on a wintry day.

'I won't stay here another day!' she insisted. 'I'm going home.'

'Without a passport?'

She stared at him blankly for a second, then it sank in, and she paled. Raphael smiled with icy mockery.

'You can't leave Greece without a passport,' he said.

She thought feverishly. 'It wasn't my fault I lost mine in the earthquake . . . I'll . . . they'll have to give me a new one!'

'That will take time. First, they'll have to investigate you back in England and make sure you are who you say you are,' he said smoothly, then before she could answer that said, 'Look, sit down, will you? You look as if you might fall down any minute.'

Annis would have argued, but he was right, she was swaying on her feet. She had come up the stairs too fast, and she was hyperventilating in her rage. She made it to a chair and subsided into it with a sigh.

'You are still very weak,' Raphael pointed out unnecessarily. 'You need a few weeks' rest and you need good care. You surely don't want to burden your poor mother with running after you at home, do you?'

Annis eyed him smoulderingly. 'It's you who blackmail me, not the other way around.'

He looked irritatingly smug. 'And you should have got your passport before we left Athens.'

'I meant to, but somehow I forgot all about it,' she stammered, then grew angry again, because why was she on the defensive when it was Raphael who should be doing all the apologising? Glaring at him, she snapped, 'I forgot because you rushed me here in such a hurry.'

'Oh, of course, it would be my fault,' he drawled.

'It usually is!' Annis threw at him.

'Harpy!' he said, his eyes suddenly smiling, and her anger died away. How could she stay furious with him when he looked at her like that?

'I'd better get in touch with the British Embassy, I suppose,' she thought aloud. 'Do I ring them? Or will I have to write? I expect I'll have to fill in forms and get a passport photo.'

'I'll find out for you,' Raphael promised calmly.

'How long will it take, though?'

He shrugged and the movement dislodged the book he had been reading, propped up on a wooden stand, which also fell to the floor with a crash. Annis jumped at the sharp noise, her nerves haywire. Ever since the night of the earthquake she had been intensely nervous of any sudden or loud noise, any unexpected event.

Raphael looked searchingly at her. 'Are you OK?'

'Yes, it was just the bang . . .' She got back on her feet, with the aid of her stick, and hobbled over to pick up the book for him.

He waved it away. 'Never mind! I find it maddening to try to turn the pages, anyway. It takes so long with my hands bandaged up like this.' He looked through his lashes, giving her a coaxing little smile and she knew what he wanted her to say, and couldn't help saying it.

'Do you want me to read to you?'

His smile curved wider. 'Would you? You know I love having you read to me. Your voice is so clear and expressive.'

She couldn't help a flush of pleasure in the compliment, especially as she knew he meant it. Raphael had always loved her to read aloud to him when he was tired or in no mood for television or music. He liked to lounge back, watching her, or with his eyes closed, while she sat next to him on a sofa or curled up on the floor by his feet, reading aloud.

A flash of memory hit her, and she inhaled, staring down at the book she held without seeing it.

The first time Raphael had kissed her had been the first time she read aloud to him. She had accompanied the orchestra on tour to Holland, to take care of all the small details of the trip. It had been a hectic time for her; she hadn't had time to breathe between getting up at crack of dawn until she fell into bed around midnight, and she had felt like a cross between a mother and a slave to most of the men in the orchestra. After the final concert there had been a party, but she had been so tired that she had left early to go back to her room, and had met Raphael in the lift. He, too, had slipped out of the party. He had been grey with exhaustion, and Annis had looked anxiously at him.

'You aren't ill, are you?' she had asked, and he had smiled wryly, shaking his head.

'Just dead on my feet!'

'You must be,' she had agreed, knowing how much he gave to each performance. 'I expect you'll be asleep before your head hits the pillow!'

He grimaced. 'I wish it were that easy! But I need to wind down first. I'm up in the stratosphere after a concert and I have to get myself back to earth before I can sleep. I shall read for an hour or so, I expect.'

They had reached his room and paused, and Raphael had looked down at her, smiling crookedly, his eyes gently pleading.

'I suppose you wouldn't read to me for a while? I find that so restful, it calms me down much faster than reading by myself.'

She had looked hesitantly at him, and he had pulled a face.

'Oh, you think it's a trick to get you into my room?'

'No,' she had protested, and the idea hadn't occurred to her.

'Well, I promise it isn't,' Raphael had said quietly.

She had believed him, and she had agreed, of course—how could she have resisted him? He had poured her champagne, they had sat close together on a couch in his room, and she had read poetry to him for half an hour, her voice soft and drowsy, her eyelids heavy, almost reading herself to sleep. Somehow she had curled up closer to him, he had pulled her head down on to his shoulder, and while she read he had played with her hair, stroking and fondling it. When she ended the last poem and looked up at him enquiringly to see if he wanted her to go on reading, he had smiled into her lifted eyes, bent down and tenderly kissed her mouth.

She had been too surprised to react, just staring at him. Raphael Leon was world-famous, an idol to his fans, deeply respected by other musicians—Annis had never expected him to take any personal interest in her. She had simply been one of the staff who worked for him, and Raphael had been surrounded by people who were eager to do anything for him.

She might, perhaps, have cynically thought, So it was a pass, after all? She might have wondered if he had been about to ask her to go to bed with him.

She hadn't. She had just blushed and looked down, shyly, and Raphael had stroked her cheek with one long, cool finger.

'You're as tired as I am, aren't you, angel? Off you go to bed, and thank you, that was very soothing, and you have a lovely voice.'

She had been so dazed that she had got back to her own room without quite knowing how, and looking back now she realised that that was the night she had fallen in love with Raphael. Was it the night he had fallen in love with her? she wondered, looking up at him.

He quizzically considered her. 'What are you thinking about now?'

She went pink. 'Nothing. I...' Her gaze wildly ran around the room and saw the open windows, the balcony outside. 'I...I was just wondering if you wanted to sit out in the sun.'

'Good idea,' he said, and she helped him to manoeuvre his chair out on to the balcony.

'Oh, by the way,' he said, as she was about to start reading, 'Melina showed me the schedule she has worked out for us to follow. We shall be getting massage and more of those special exercises we had in hospital.'

Annis started to laugh helplessly, and he stared at her, his brows rising.

'What's so funny?'

'Everything,' she said. 'Here we are, alone together, on this marvellous island—it ought to be romantic, the dream of a lifetime. Instead, we sit here talking about exercises and massages.'

'Disappointed?' he drawled, mouth wry.

'Relieved, in fact,' Annis said defiantly, at once—and it was almost true. It ought to be true, anyway. She should be very relieved that she was in no danger of Raphael's turning on the heat in this dreamy setting, and it annoyed her that there was one tiny, idiotic part of her that felt a pang of disappointment.

Raphael considered her, his head to one side. 'Hmm. I'm not sure I believe you. Anyway, we aren't just going to be lazing about here, if Melina means what she says, and I have a sinking feeling she does! That girl has all the makings of a tyrant. I wonder why all nurses are born dictators?'

'It comes with the job,' Annis said, raising the book. 'Shall I start reading now?'

'Please,' he said, settling comfortably like a little boy whose mother was going to read him a story, and Annis began.

They had lunch at midday, simple and delicious Greek food: a cold aubergine starter followed by lamb kebabs and salad with rice and then fruit. Melina made them both rest after lunch. At three she gave Annis her massage and then they all did exercises, largely stretching and bending ones which Raphael could do even in his wheelchair.

It was a surprise to Annis to realise how rapidly the day had gone by—they had hardly relaxed after their exercises than it was time for dinner. Again, it was simple but beautifully cooked.

'I love Greek food,' she told Melina. 'It must be easy to diet here. Everything is grilled or barbecued, and served with salad or rice.'

'So long as you don't get addicted to honey cakes!' Melina grinned at her.

They all sat out on the terrace after dinner that evening, watching the sun sink slowly behind the trees and listening to the cicadas.

It was a magical hour, and Annis found herself slipping into a sort of trance, her body utterly relaxed, her mind drifting back, sifting through memories she had tried so hard to forget but which had never lost their power.

The gentle beginning of her relationship with Raphael had melted into a passionate affair, mind and body, and as she had got to know him intimately she had realised how complex a man she had met. Tender one minute, fierce the next; a wild, explosive lover, a kind and caring friend. Every day she had seemed to see a new facet of his personality, some of them disturbing.

Once when he had got back a day early from one of his tours, he'd arrived at her flat at midnight just in time to see a strange man leaving. Annis hadn't had time to explain. She had opened the door when the bell rang furiously, and Raphael had burst in on her, his eyes like hot coals, snarling, 'Who is he?'

Confused, she had backed, staring. 'What? What are you talking about——?'

'Don't try to lie! I saw him leave your flat!' he had grated in a harsh voice she didn't recognise. 'How long has it been going on? Is it new, or have you been seeing him behind my back all along?'

Dazedly, she had realised what was behind the outburst, and had said in a shaking voice, 'Oh... Jack...you mean Jack——'

'I don't care what his damned name is, you lying little cheat!' he had snapped, grabbing her arms and shaking her violently, and she had been frightened by the look in his face.

But then from the doorway of her bedroom a nervous little voice had said, 'Jack's my boyfriend, Mr Leon.'

Raphael's head had swung round, he had let go of Annis and stared blankly at one of the typists from the office. Tracy, small and fluffy-haired, just eighteen, had given him a worried smile. 'I'm staying the night with Annis because I missed my last train home. Jack and I had been to see a play and we had supper, and it got so late...and I rang Annis and she said it was OK to stay the night, so Jack brought me round, and then he went...'

'I see,' Raphael had said, darkly flushed and frowning.

'It's OK, Tracy,' Annis had said. 'Off you go to bed.'

Tracy had gratefully ducked out of the room, closing the door, and Raphael had looked down at Annis, his mouth crooked.

'Do you hate me? What on earth can I say? Jumping to conclusions... I should have known you weren't the cheating type....'

'You should,' she had said, disturbed by the violence he had just shown her.

He had lifted her hands to his mouth, kissed them with bent dark head, his mouth lingering. 'I saw the guy come out, you see, and it was like being stabbed, this jealousy... I didn't stop to think, to ask myself if you would cheat me...I just went mad. I'm sorry, Annis...forgive me for being such a fool.'

She hadn't been able to be angry for long; she had smiled, because his jealousy did, at least, mean that he must really love her very deeply, and when she had lifted her face to him he'd kissed her, framing her face between hands that shook.

That moment had changed something between them; a darkness had been revealed between them, a hunger, a piercing need. She had felt him trembling against her, had felt the heat in his skin as she touched him.

'I was afraid you were sleeping with someone else,' he had muttered roughly. 'That's the truth, my darling. I seem to have waited for centuries to get you into bed. I'm going out of my head with frustration and, seeing another man leaving here, I thought...Oh, it was crazy, I know you aren't a cheat, but I love you, and I want you. I can't bear this much longer, Annis. If you insist on waiting until we're married, at least marry me at once.'

It hadn't been easy, though; his schedule had been so heavily booked up in advance and her family would have had to fly over to England to be at the wedding. They had spent hours with his engagement diary in front of them, trying to fit their wedding in among the concerts and tours, and in the end, of course, she had fled long before the day arrived.

But hadn't she used her knowledge of his jealous uncertainty when she'd written that letter telling him it was over, she was going away with another man? Raphael might be famous and sought-after, but he had exposed his doubts about himself, his inner fear of losing her, and so she had known that he would believe her lie about loving someone else.

Melina yawned suddenly, getting to her feet, which broke the dreamy spell of the Greek night, and Annis came back to the present to stare blankly around her.

'Were you asleep in your chair?' Melina asked cheerfully. 'Well, so was I, almost, and it's time for bed, I think, don't you?'

Raphael was watching Annis, his eyes half closed. She glanced at him, flushed, and avoided those eyes. What was he thinking? She wondered if he had been watching her all the time while she had been lost in the past, remembering the way it had been between them. Had her face betrayed her thoughts?

How much longer could she stand it here, in this dangerous, heart-wrenching intimacy with him?

At noon next day the serpent returned to Eden. Annis heard the car arrive and looked down from her bedroom window to see Diona Munthe sauntering up the terrace steps with a come-hither smile on her face which told

Annis that Raphael was downstairs to greet the new arrival.

'Darling!' Diona purred, and through her open window Annis distinctly caught the sound of a kiss. She slammed the window shut and sat down to stare at herself in the dressing-table mirror. Her face was taut, her blue eyes like knives, her skin hot.

How was she going to put up with Diona Munthe around all the time? She knew the type only too well. She had seen them so often in the past—predatory music buffs or professional singers eager to get close to one of the leading composers of the day. They had always clustered around Raphael, and at the moment he was in no condition to run away, even if he wanted to! In that wheelchair, he was literally a sitting target.

Annis would have been jealous of any woman who tried to get too close to Raphael, but if she had been sure the other woman loved him as much as she did, if she thought Raphael could be happier with someone else, she would have gritted her teeth and borne it. But she didn't believe for one second that Diona was serious about Raphael, or really cared for him. She was merely an ambitious opportunist. Raphael was influential in the music world; he could write Diona wonderful music and he could introduce her to people she would find useful.

Annis made her slow way downstairs, leaning on her stick, growing more and more impatient of her plaster cast, and met Melina, looking very bad-tempered. She could always tell when Melina was cross; her black brows seemed to grow thicker and blacker and her mouth became a tight line.

'She's here!' she hissed at Annis, who pulled a face.

'I know. I saw her from my window.'

'She dismissed me!' seethed Melina, red spots in her cheeks. 'With a wave of her hand, like a duchess! ''Run

along, Nurse," she said. "We don't need you." Oh!'
Her hands became little claws and she breathed fer-
ociously. 'How I would love to——' She broke off as
Annis laughed. 'This is not funny!'

'No, but you are! Your expression! Not that I don't
agree with you, but don't let her get you worked up,
Melina! She isn't worth it.'

Melina considered that, then nodded. 'You are right.
She isn't worth it. Oh, but men are such fools! Mr Leon
is sitting there with a happy smile on his face while she
kneels by his chair flattering him and treating him like
a god, and he does not seem to realise she does not mean
a word of it. Why can't he see through her? Is he blind?
He cannot be so stupid!'

'There are always women like her round him,' Annis
said flatly, her face blank although she was eaten with
jealousy over Melina's description of Raphael and Diona
together. 'Everywhere he goes, women chuck themselves at him and don't care how blatantly they're be-
having. He's had years to get used to it; he probably
expects that adoration now.' He couldn't have been surprised when she, herself, had fallen for him. He hadn't
acted as if he was unsure of himself, anyway. What was
surprising was merely that Raphael had wanted her!

Melina stared at her, curiosity in her dark eyes. 'You
two puzzle me. You never flatter him or treat him like
someone famous. Sometimes you seem so happy
together...'

Annis blushed helplessly, looking away.

'And then at other times you seem to hate each other.'
She paused and Annis knew she was waiting for some
explanation—but what on earth could she say?

She shrugged. Sooner or later, Melina was bound to
work out the truth, so why not tell her? 'We've known
each other a long time,' she said flatly, turning away,

and went out on to the terrace to find Raphael lying on a cushioned lounger, his head pillowed, his long, lean body totally relaxed, while beside him Diona was stretched out on another lounger, lazily sipping a pink-champagne cocktail.

Raphael turned his mocking grey eyes towards Annis, watching her carefully arranged blank expression. She knew she was not fooling him—his amused smile told her as much—but she ignored him. It was Diona she wanted to deceive. The singer gave her a cold glance as she sat down.

'You met Annis yesterday, didn't you?' said Raphael, and Diona nodded distantly. Annis nodded back, pouring herself a glass of the iced lemonade on the table.

'Do you want a champagne cocktail?' asked Raphael. 'Irena will be back with some in a moment.'

Annis shook her head. 'No, thanks, iced lemonade is perfect in this heat.' And she needed to have a clear head for the next few hours, with Diona Munthe around.

'So are you going to the Swedish festival?' Diona asked Raphael, her tone excluding Annis from the conversation.

'That will depend on how long it takes me to recover!' he said drily.

Diona made a dove-like cooing sound. 'Oh, poor Raphael! And you can't even play the piano! How lucky that you can still compose. If you need someone to write your music down for you I'd be honoured to help.'

'I don't think I'm in the writing mood, but thanks for the offer!' Diona started to talk about her own work: operas she had sung in, festivals at which she had appeared, her favourite songs, her favourite composers.

Annis sat by the table, totally ignored by the other woman, to whom, it seemed, she was invisible. Diona was only interested in Raphael, and clearly did not care

what Annis thought of her. Annis listened without surprise to the revelation of an enormous ego, wondering
what Raphael made of it. Raphael showed no signs of
surprise either, or of disapproval. As she had said to
Melina, he was used to women like Diona, especially
singers like Diona, whose own careers were the only thing
that mattered in the world. Raphael even seemed to be
enjoying Diona's avalanche of self-publicity. It appealed
to his sense of humour.

Irena came out a quarter of an hour later to tell them
that lunch was ready. Diona insisted on pushing
Raphael's wheelchair along the wide terrace to where a
large table was laid for three. Usually Melina joined
them, but Annis saw that she had opted out of this particular meal, which meant that it was Annis who cut up
Raphael's food for him.

'I'll do that!' Diona said, leaning over to snatch the
knife and fork out of her hand.

Raphael intervened smoothly. 'No, no, I want you to
enjoy your meal, not wait on me!'

Diona looked at him through her long, black, blatantly
artificial lashes. 'Darling, you're so thoughtful!' Her
sideways glance dismissed Annis. Raphael had put her
in a bracket Diona could understand. Annis was there
to wait on him; she was of no importance whatever, after
all.

Annis went on cutting up Raphael's food, her teeth
tight-set, not that either of the other two seemed to
notice. Diona talked to Raphael alone, openly flirting,
giving him intimate smiles, a touch of the hand to em-
phasise something, flicking a finger along his cheek when
he made a joke. Annis pretended not to notice; she ate
in silence, her eyes on her food, an ache deep inside her.
Diona was so beautiful, they had so much more in
common—how could Annis not be jealous?

She kept remembering other times when this had happened—when she had found herself isolated at a dinner party, where all the other guests were in the music world and the women were competing for Raphael's attention. She always felt so inadequate on those occasions. What did she have to offer a man like Raphael, after all? She was so ordinary, so dull and quiet, without any special talent.

The meal seemed endless to Annis, but at last Irena served their coffee. Annis helped Raphael lift his cup to his mouth, and he eyed her quizzically as their eyes met. 'You're very quiet.'

She gave him an ironic glance. What else did he expect when Diona monopolised him? she thought, but all she said was, 'Am I?'

Diona gave one of her operatic trills of laughter, grating on Annis's ear. 'Darling, don't embarrass her!' She pretended to smile at Annis, strictly for Raphael's benefit. 'We should have remembered that we were talking over her head! It's been such fun for us, but shop talk is so boring for outsiders, isn't it?'

A hard flush crawled up Annis's face at that. She had always felt an outsider, but Diona was the first person to put it into words, and it stung.

'Have you been bored, Annis?' Raphael asked, and her angry eyes answered for her, appearing to amuse him. Raphael was enjoying this chance to torment her, especially as she was impotent to do anything about it in front of Diona.

Melina appeared like a jack out of a box. 'Time for your rest!' she brightly announced, and he pulled a face at Diona.

'I have my orders, you see! I'm no longer a free man.'

'Get rid of both of them, darling!' Diona said, in a honeyed voice, pretending to smile as she bent to kiss him. Annis knew how often theatre people kissed, but this was different. It was a lingering and sensual kiss on the mouth, and Annis looked away rather than watch, rage smouldering inside her. Melina was irritated, too; she jerked the wheelchair away suddenly, forcing Diona to break off the kiss, and the opera singer went red.

Melina and Raphael vanished, but Diona was in a bad temper now. She glared at Annis, demanding, 'Well? Have you thought over my offer?'

Annis nodded coolly, getting to her feet. 'Yes, I thought about it, and the answer is no,' she said, beginning to walk slowly away.

Diona's mouth took on an ugly curve. Her slim foot suddenly shot out as Annis took another careful step, and the next second Annis felt herself stumble and begin to fall. She gave a wild cry of shock and fear.

CHAPTER SEVEN

ANNIS was very lucky. A few inches the wrong way and she would have fallen on the marble floor and might well have ended up back in hospital, which was probably what Diona Munthe had intended! But as she fell Annis realised the danger and threw herself sideways to fall across one of the cushioned loungers standing around the terrace.

All the same, she landed with an impact which knocked all the breath out of her, and lay there, winded for a moment, too shaken to notice what Diona did.

Then Melina was there, anxiously helping her to her feet, gabbling, 'What on earth happened? Did you hurt yourself? Are you in pain?'

'No, I think I'm OK,' Annis said uncertainly, still off balance after the fall. 'I had a soft landing!' she added with an attempt at humour which only got a worried look from Melina's dark eyes.

'But how did you fall? Did you trip?'

Annis looked around the terrace, not very surprised to find that Diona had vanished. 'Yes, I tripped,' she said grimly. Diona Munthe was some sort of lunatic. Surely she couldn't have meant to do serious damage? Or could she? 'Where has Diona gone?' she asked, and Melina looked over her shoulder, down the steps to the drive.

'There's her car leaving now!' she said with unhidden satisfaction. 'I guessed that as soon as Mr Leon had gone, she would go too, thank heavens. You had better come up to your room and lie down.'

'Raphael said you were a tyrant, and he's right!' Annis teased.

'Did he really say that? Well, I want him to be scared of me—it's the only way I can get him to behave himself. He'll be wanting to run before he can walk, and it's essential if he is ever to walk properly again that he listens to me.'

Annis frowned, anxiety in her blue eyes. 'Is there any danger that he may not walk properly again?'

'After breaking both legs? Of course. It's very important for him to be patient, and to do the correct exercises to keep his muscles in good shape even though he can't walk. He knows I'm right, but like most men he lacks patience.'

'And he gets scared of the future at times!' said Annis protectively, her heart wrung at the thought of Raphael unable to walk or play the piano.

Melina smiled at her. 'We mustn't let him brood over what may never happen. He has to learn to take life day by day. You know, Annis, I am very glad you are here. You will make my work much easier just by being on hand to keep him cheerful and occupied. He needs you.'

Annis wished she hadn't said that. It was hard enough to decide whether to stay on here or leave without Melina landing her with the responsibility for Raphael's eventual recovery.

'What about his hands?' she slowly asked. 'Do you know what his chances are?'

'Nobody knows. Tendons are tricky; the operation sometimes works, sometimes doesn't. You can't predict the outcome. Oh, he will be able to use his hands for most things, but whether or not he will ever be able to play the piano the way he once did is anybody's guess. I shouldn't imagine even his surgeon would like to bet on it.'

Annis gave a long sigh, her face sombre. 'If he can't give any more concerts, it will break his heart.'

'Then we must hope the operation worked, mustn't we?' Melina said calmly. Annis looked at her, and envied her that fatalistic acceptance. It was probably what Melina needed to do her job, but it was an attitude Annis could not take towards Raphael's chances of playing again. She cared too deeply, and she knew that after what Melina had said she was not going to leave Raphael to bear the next few weeks alone. She had to stay with him until he found out whether or not his hands were going to recover their elasticity, and whether or not he was going to walk properly again.

She went up to her room and slept for an hour on her bed, with the shutters over her windows closed and blue shadows creeping across the room in the somnolent heat of the Greek afternoon.

She woke up abruptly from a terrifying dream of being trapped, her mouth full of dust, her eyes blind. Sitting up, heart pounding, she stared around the room, so confused for a moment that she didn't know where she was, and then she remembered and relief flooded into her. She swung herself off the bed, perspiration trickling down her body, and limped to the bathroom to wash her face, neck and hands in cool water.

She had been dreaming about the earthquake, of course—and yet, on another level, it had been that recurring dream with which she had lived for so long. In the workshop of the mind all her experiences were put together in a new way, and she kept reliving them, trying to make sense of those muddled memories. Perhaps if she could talk about it, bring it out into the open, she might start to forget. But who could she trust? She dared not take the risk of confiding in anyone.

At dinner that evening, Melina asked uncertainly, 'Would you object if I took a few hours off tonight? I...want to meet someone.'

Annis grinned at her. 'A date? Is he handsome?'

Melina was rather pink. '*I* think so,' she said, her Greek accent thicker than usual because she was feeling shy.

'You're entitled to an evening off,' said Raphael.

'Thank you. I will be back by ten, before you go to bed,' Melina promised, and left while they were drinking their Greek coffee on the terrace, watching the moon drifting through the dark blue summer sky.

'Music?' Annis asked Raphael, who nodded. She selected some of his favourite Chopin pieces and they sat listening for half an hour without talking. It was a peaceful interlude, quietly happy.

'I had a phone call from Barry tonight,' he said suddenly, and she stared at him, her face tense.

'Carmel isn't worse?'

'No, it wasn't that, but almost as worrying. He wanted to borrow money. He said he needed a new car but hadn't enough in his bank account, but I got the feeling he was lying—I'm not sure why. I don't really trust him, Annis, and that's disturbing. Carmel has enough problems without her husband's adding to them!'

Annis stared out over the moonlit gardens. 'She depends on him, doesn't she?'

'More every day as the illness takes a stronger hold,' Raphael said sombrely. 'They have a woman to clean the house and help out with the children, and a nurse comes in for a few hours every day to take care of Carmel herself, and Barry still works six days a week, putting in pretty long hours when he's busy—but when Carmel has her bad days Barry has to stay home and take charge of everything.'

'But you don't like him much, do you?' Annis said slowly.

Raphael made a face. 'You always were shrewd about things like that! No, I never did like Barry—he and I are chalk and cheese. But the marriage hasn't been easy on him, and he doesn't complain—at least not to me! He's been a tower of strength to her.' He laughed shortly. 'I didn't want Carmel to get married at that age, I thought she was far too young, but I wouldn't have been so worried if she had picked some other guy. I knew I was never going to like Barry. He was too smooth, too street-smart for me. He can sell a car to anyone, and he can talk his way out of anything, but I don't happen to find those particularly admirable characteristics. Oh, I know a lot of people who think he's charming. But usually they're women, not men!' He gave her a sideways look, his grey eyes acute. 'You, though...you never liked him from the start either, did you?'

She shook her head, her lips compressed.

'Why?' Raphael asked curiously.

She shrugged. 'Instinct, I suppose. I had nothing to go on then...'

Raphael's eyes narrowed. 'Now you have?'

'Now that I've got to know him, yes,' she said quickly, aware of an uneasy flush creeping up her face. 'My instincts are usually quite reliable.'

'Female intuition,' murmured Raphael, frowning to himself. 'A pity Carmel didn't have any. I've never known what she saw in him.'

'Love has its own reasoning,' Annis said sadly.

'Reason has nothing to do with love,' Raphael corrected, mouth hard.

She got up to change the disc they were playing. It took a long time for her to walk across the terrace into the spacious lounge, change the disc, and walk back as

Tchaikovsky's piano music passionately swelled up into the quiet air. When she got back to the terrace Raphael had his eyes closed, his head back against the cushioned back of his lounger. She halted beside him, frowning. Was he asleep? Should she turn the music off? A little breeze came out of nowhere and blew his black hair across his face, making his brows meet. He instinctively put up a bandaged hand to brush the hair back, then gave an angry little groan as he remembered how little he could do with his hands at the moment.

Annis felt her heart contract with pity. Raphael's hands had always been the centre of his existence; they were such beautiful hands, long fingered, elegant, powerful. It must be devastating for him to be unable to use them.

She quickly leaned over to push the black strands away from his face and he opened his eyes to look up at her, then, before she could straighten up again, he had encircled her waist with his arms.

Her breathing went haywire. 'Don't!' she muttered, trying to wriggle free without hurting him.

He leaned his head forward and with a shock she felt his mouth against her throat. She closed her eyes, trembling. 'Raphael, stop it,' she said with a pretence of anger, grasping his arms with careful fingers to try to prise them apart. Since she was afraid to use any real pressure she couldn't budge them; indeed, they seemed to tighten on her waist, and meanwhile his mouth grew heated, browsed urgently along her skin, moved down to her scooped neckline, pushed the thin cotton material aside and found her breasts.

Annis gave a sharp cry of helpless pleasure as he burrowed down into the valley between them. Her hands came up and caught his black head. She meant to push him away, but as her fingers closed on his thick, smooth hair the feel of it on her skin made her go weak with love and need. The music rose irresistibly, and so did the emotions she had been fighting for so long. She cradled his head in her palms, letting her fingertips dive down into the warm, black hair, stroking and winnowing, watching little blue sparks of electricity from their contact flash in the dusk. Raphael's mouth was following the full, aching curve of her breasts, discovering what the thin cotton had no doubt made evident to him—that she wore no bra. She had not worn one since the earthquake because it was too painful to have straps pressing down on her bruised shoulders.

Somehow Raphael had managed to push her dress down so far that his lips found her nipples. The soft teasing of his tongue made her move restlessly, desire burning deep inside her, but at the same time she felt an almost maternal tenderness for this man whose head was at her breast, seeking the comfort of her body.

He was as helpless as a baby; he couldn't walk a step, he couldn't even get up without assistance, and she knew he was in constant pain. All her female instincts conspired against her. She didn't stop him taking her nipples in his mouth; she stroked his hair and murmured softly, inaudibly, soothingly. How could she deny him anything he needed when he was in pain?

She bent and kissed his temples, and his head finally fell back against the cushions, his arms let go of her waist and he looked at her with dark-eyed weariness, swearing under his breath. 'Who am I kidding? I'm not up to making love to you yet—I'm still as weak as a kitten.'

Her mouth quivered tenderly. 'Poor Raphael!'

'Don't you laugh at me, woman!' he said, grey eyes glittering. 'Wait until I'm on my feet, and then we'll see who laughs!'

She bent quickly and kissed his mouth, felt his lips cling, grow urgent, demanding. Annis pulled free and stood up, very flushed. Raphael lay there, watching her with unnerving intensity as she went back to her own lounger and lay down. She was still shuddering with aroused desire, her skin hot, her body aching for his, but she kept her face averted to hide from him how she felt.

She was angry at her own folly. She had known the risks. How had she let it happen? She should never have gone anywhere near him, never been alone with him. This was a dangerous atmosphere: moonlight, the scent of flowers, the warm air, the seductive silence. It was a trap and she had walked right into it. Now she had betrayed herself.

Raphael was silent for what seemed an eternity, then he said huskily, 'When are you going to tell me the truth, Annis?'

She bit her lip and didn't answer because she was afraid that whatever she said would merely betray her even more. Raphael waited for a moment, then said, 'You lied, didn't you?'

Again the silence, and he went on, 'There is no other man. Is there? There never was one. You lied to me to cover the real reason why you were going. So, if you didn't leave me for someone else, why did you run out on me? Why won't you tell me? It can't be so bad that you can't talk about it!'

She couldn't speak, and after a pause he asked thoughtfully, 'Can it? Whatever it was, I might be able to help if I knew. Perhaps you haven't thought it out clearly. Tell me, Annis. Let me try to help, at least.'

'No,' she said at last, her voice drained and tired. 'I can't. Please, Raphael, let it go. There's nothing to be done. It's just one of those things. Please. Forget about it.'

'Forget about it?' he threw back harshly, and she saw his eyes glitter in the shadows of the terrace. 'Forget about it? How do I do that, Annis? I've tried, believe me. Oh, I've tried! I tried to forget about you for two years, and I never succeeded. You walked out on me when I was deeply in love with you. That never happened to me before in my life. I didn't know anything could hurt that way. It was like being dropped from a great height. You don't bounce back after a fall like that. You're left in a great many pieces, and, like Humpty Dumpty, not all the King's horses and all the King's men can put you together again.'

Her eyes glistened with tears she tried vainly to hold back. 'Raphael, don't——'

'Don't what?' he interrupted fiercely. 'Don't remind you what you did to me? You're full of glib advice, Annis. Forget it, you said—sorry, but it's just one of those things, let it go. Well, I can't let it go. Forgetting isn't that easy. Or maybe it is for you. Did you forget me?'

She stiffened, going white but still saying nothing, and Raphael laughed with a bitter satisfaction. 'No. You didn't, did you? For all your bland talk about forgetting, you couldn't get me out of your head, any more than I could get you out of mine. You can't have loved me, or you wouldn't have dumped me. No woman could do that to a man if she really cared about him. But you couldn't simply wipe me out of your memory either, could you? That's been obvious ever since we walked into each other again in that hotel in Athens. I knew almost at once that there was unfinished business between us. It was crackling in the air, like a leak of electricity.'

The moon passed behind clouds, plunging the garden into darkness, thickening the shadows on the terrace, which was lit only by ironwork lamps, one on each side of the main door.

Their soft glow, masked by amber glass, did not reach far, but dusky moths fluttered around them, infatuated by the golden light, as unable to stay away from it as she was unable to stay away from Raphael.

'You still want me, don't you, Annis?' he whispered in that husky, intimate voice. 'Just now, you wanted me; do you think I can't tell? Is that all there ever was between us? Did you just want me? And not only in bed, either. Did you want everything else I stand for—the money, the fame, all that? I'm always meeting women who want me for what they think I am, rather than for myself. They come on as soon as I've shaken hands, throwing themselves at me just because I'm a public name, a public face. It's just a performance, I don't mean anything real to them. What was I to you, Annis? A trophy? Did you give me a private and personal performance to win your own Oscar?'

She put her hands over her ears. 'Stop it. Stop it.'

He was full of hatred, bitterness; and yet when he kissed her there had been such passion and feeling between them. The darkness hid her face, concealing from him the tears which had begun to spill down her cheeks. She put a hand over her mouth so that he shouldn't hear her cry.

There was a silence, then he said brusquely, 'Don't!'

She hadn't made a sound, was barely breathing, but somehow he knew.

'Stop crying!' he muttered angrily, and she swallowed and cleared her throat before she answered him.

'I'm not.'

'Don't lie!' he said furiously. 'You're a bad liar. I always know you're lying. And I always hate it when you cry, but I hate it most of all when you cry silently. That really tears me up, do you know that? Do you know? Is that why you do it? Do you want to put me through a wringer? Well, stop it, damn you. Stop it!'

Suddenly a beam of light fell across the terrace, like a searchlight in a prisoner-of-war camp, illuminating his angry face, the face of the enemy, showing her the grey eyes glittering, the mouth fierce and bitter. She stiffened, her wet eyes wide with shock, staring at him without understanding for a moment where the light was coming from. Then she realised that the darkness had been split by a car's headlights. Relief welled up in her. Melina was back!

Raphael laughed ironically. 'Just in time! You must be overjoyed to see her.'

Annis reached for her stick and began to get up. She was bone-tired, aching with exhaustion.

'That's it, run away again,' he mocked.

She slowly limped to the door. 'Goodnight, Raphael!'

'Pleasant dreams,' he called softly, a tormenting malice in his voice, and she winced. She knew what he meant—that she should dream about him.

If he only knew what she did dream about! Ever since the earthquake the nightmare had been back, and now she had it almost every night. If she could tell anyone about it, it might stop coming, but she couldn't. It lay always at the bottom of her mind, out of sight of the daylight, crawling out at night when she was at her weakest, when she was most vulnerable to those hidden fears.

During the days that followed, Annis made quite sure that she was rarely alone with Raphael, and never at night. On Melina's night off, Annis went up to her room,

pleading sleepiness, and although Raphael looked ironically at her he didn't argue or try to stop her, perhaps
because neither of them wanted to wreck their precari-
ously balanced relationship while they were both so weak.

They were kept busy following the daily schedule
Melina had worked out, and most days Diona Munthe
visited Raphael. Annis steered clear of her—partly because Diona made it plain she did not want Annis
around, and partly because Annis did not want to see
Diona flirting with Raphael. She knew Raphael admired
Diona's talent. She had a miraculous voice and a
considerable stage presence. The two of them talked
music endlessly when they were together, and that was
something from which Annis was necessarily excluded.
She loved music, but it was not her life, her whole existence, as it was for Diona and Raphael. They were
professionals, she wasn't, and her jealousy of the other
woman was worse than ever when she overheard them
talking in that casual, intimate way about things in which
she could have no part.

She walked in on them one day and found Diona at
the piano in the enormous lounge, playing music Annis
had never heard, but which she guessed at once was by
Raphael.

Annis halted in the doorway, jealousy jabbing at her.
Was this something new? Something he was composing
for Diona? Raphael was sitting on a chair beside Diona,
his head close to hers; Annis heard him humming the
music the singer was playing. Diona stopped playing,
looked up at him, face flushed, excited.

'Darling, this is exactly the music I imagined for the
poems! Oh, you're so wonderful!' She leaned over to
kiss him and Raphael leaned towards her to meet the
kiss.

Annis went out as quietly as she had come in, knowing that neither of them was even aware of her. She wished she could get away now. She felt so shut out and so lonely. She began to count the days until they were due to have their plaster casts removed. Her leg itched unbearably, and she was sick of dragging about, leaning on a stick; and as for Raphael, his irritability and black moods were growing worse every day, except when he and Diona were working at the piano together. Then he seemed much more cheerful, and that hurt Annis even more.

One evening, a few days before they were to fly back to Athens to see the specialist, Raphael and Diona spent hours talking music, ignoring Annis. It was too early to go to bed, and she was tired of sitting in her bedroom. She sat obstinately on the terrace staring at the midnight-blue sky, counting stars and resenting every word the other two said.

'When you're better, we must get together!' said Diona, her eyes provocative, full of sexual invitation, making it clear she did not just mean to work. 'It's an exciting idea, a concert. You would play one of your sonatas, and I would sing your new songs. I'm so thrilled with them. I've always loved those poems—this is what you should have been writing all along, something ultramodern, dramatic.' She smiled happily. 'Perfect for my voice. You and I were meant to come together.'

'I'm beginning to think maybe we were,' Raphael said.

Annis went on staring at the stars, holding her body tautly, trying to hide the jealousy and pain tearing through her. If they had started working together, it would mean having Diona permanently in his life, and it was obvious that Diona did not want just a professional relationship. What would Raphael do about that? Give her what she wanted, to keep her happy?

When Diona had left at last, Raphael gave Annis a harsh stare, his brows together. 'Do you have to be so damned rude?'

The injustice took her breath away. For a second she could only flounder like a fish out of water, her mouth open.

'Me, rude?' she stammered at last, dark red in the face. 'Me? I sit here night after night while you and that...that...singer...jabber away together and treat me as if I were the invisible woman! Then you call me rude?'

'You never even attempt to join in the conversation!'

'How can I when the two of you rarely even pause for breath? You never talk about anything but music.'

'You used to tell me you loved music too!'

'I do, but you and Diona don't talk about it on my level. I enjoy listening to music, but I'm just one of the audience. I don't know most of these people you talk about, and I'm not involved in whatever you're working on with her at the moment. I don't understand the finer points of a score, I can't follow what you're saying, and Diona Munthe knows that. She looks at me triumphantly and smiles that catty little smile of hers——'

Raphael's eyes gleamed and his mouth curved. 'You don't need to be jealous of her, Annis,' he said in a soft, husky voice. 'She's a colleague, don't you understand? We are working together, and she's a damn good musician. She knows what makes a score work; she has a fine sense of the way words and music have to fit together. Oh, surely you can see...if she were a man I talked shop with, would that bother you?'

'But she isn't a man, is she?' muttered Annis. Diona Munthe was a sensual and dangerous woman prepared to use any weapon, including her body, to promote her

career, and Raphael must know she was stalking him
night after night. Sooner or later she would close in for
the kill—and what would Raphael do then?

Diona had so much more in common with him than
Annis had ever had, and she was far more strikingly
lovely than Annis could ever be—why shouldn't he prefer
Diona? Annis had never understood why Raphael had
chosen her in the first place. She knew she was just an
ordinary girl, a home-maker, not a glamorous star. She
wouldn't be amazed if Raphael had begun to realise that
what he really needed as a wife was a woman from his
own world!

CHAPTER EIGHT

MELINA woke Annis very late next morning, pulling back the curtains to let sunlight flood over the bed. Annis yawned and groaned, reluctantly opened her eyes and struggled up against her pillows.

'Breakfast in bed,' Melina said, smiling cheerfully, a tray in her hands.

'What time is it?' Annis looked at her clock, and groaned. 'Oh, you shouldn't have let me sleep!'

'Why not?' Melina said indulgently. 'You're supposed to be on holiday. Hop out of bed and go to the bathroom, then you can get back in bed and eat your breakfast.'

Annis swung her legs out, grasped her stick and set off on the trek across the room. She was back in a couple of minutes, her face washed and shining, her long, blonde hair well brushed and held in place by a wide pale blue headband of silk ribbon.

'Now, eat your breakfast,' said Melina. 'I must go and get Raphael up. He slept late this morning, too. What did you two get up to last night?'

She turned away as she said that, laughing, and so she did not see Annis flush hotly. Melina had been joking, of course. She was a nurse; she knew the idea of them 'getting up' to anything was ludicrous, in their condition, but the mere suggestion made Annis acutely self-conscious.

She picked up her coffee-cup as Melina left the room, and sipped, staring out of the window at that lustrous Greek sky. Light was what everybody mentioned when they talked about Greece, and she could see why. Her eyes dazzled in that radiance; she felt she could see for a thousand miles in any direction. She wished she could see her way in life as clearly.

A light tap on her door made her start, looking round. Raphael faced her, leaning on two sticks. He had become quite agile with them lately, and Annis smiled at his self-congratulatory expression.

'You'll be able to run with those things soon!' she said and Raphael grinned.

'Think I could play golf with them?'

'You wouldn't be able to use a golf-club, though.'

'I could use these as clubs!' He leaned on one stick and demonstrated with the other.

She laughed but said anxiously, 'Be careful, Raphael!'

He straightened his body, leaning on both sticks again, watching her with warm grey eyes. 'You look like Alice in Wonderland with that band in your long, fair hair and that blue nightie!'

Annis made a rueful face. 'I always hated that book when I was a little girl. It scared me.'

'I expect you hated the nonsense element,' he said. 'The lack of logic, everything upside-down. I can see that that would bother you. You're one of the organisers of the world; you like everything in its proper place. You like to arrange life neatly, don't you? You have a strong sense of order.'

'You make me sound very boring,' she said unhappily. Was that really how he saw her?

'Boring?' he repeated, mouth wry. 'No, I wouldn't call you boring, Annis! You're too unpredictable. One minute you're strictly practical and down to earth, and the next you're dewy-eyed and romantic. There's no way of guessing what you'll do next.' His eyes hardened. 'I hadn't expected you to vanish out of my life without warning, for instance...'

She bit her lip, looking away. Oh, if only there were some way for her to tell Raphael the truth. She could be wrong about the way he would react. He might not erupt like a volcano and bring all their lives down around their ears. If she talked quietly to him, made him see...

'Why did you leave me?' he asked abruptly, making her jump. He often surprised her by tuning into her thoughts in a partial, fragmentary way, not reading her mind so much as being somehow, mysteriously, aware what she was thinking about.

When she didn't answer, he said soberly, 'Did my way of life put you off?' and for the first time she realised that that had, actually, been part of it.

'It isn't easy for an ordinary woman to cope with being married to a very famous man,' she said quietly, and he grimaced.

'It isn't easy for a very ordinary man to cope with being famous.'

She stared, startled, and he went on, 'I wasn't always famous, you know. It happened quite fast and it takes a while to get used to! And, on top of that, musicians live restlessly and untidily even when they're successful. I realised you hated it when I had to keep going away— you were always depressed and nervous before I went— but it's part of the job. What could I do about it? I don't know that I enjoy it much myself, now. When I was younger I did—I loved all the travelling and coming and going, living in suitcases, in hotels, never in one place for long. As I got older, it no longer seemed such great fun. I was very relieved to have my home to go back to, I'd never have sold that house, you know. We would always have had the Manchester house for our base, and when children came along you could have stayed with them while I travelled, or come along, just as you liked.'

She gave him a quick look, and saw the fierce bone-structure, the glitter of grey eyes, the hardness of jawline and mouth.

'I know I'm selfish, wanting to have both you and my music,' he said huskily. 'If I could change my way of life for you, I would, believe me...but I can't, you know that. I can't compromise on my music.'

'I know you can't,' she said, a sigh wrenching her. Raphael had never been able to compromise. She knew what would happen if she told him the real reason why she had had to break their engagement; he would be too angry to care about the consequences.

They both heard Melina calling him. 'Breakfast is on the terrace!'

Raphael grinned at Annis. 'Will you come down soon?'

'I think I may stay in bed today,' she said, avoiding his eyes.

He was silent, staring hard. Then he said harshly, 'Do as you damn well please, then!'

The door slammed. Annis stared at where he had been, her eyes full of tears. No, she dared not even think about telling him the truth. Raphael was too explosive. It was too big a risk. She had to stop daydreaming, shut off that aching need. But how did you do that when you were sick with love?

Think about something else, she ordered herself. Anything else. What, though? The weather? She made a wryly amused face. What could one say about the weather here? In England, where you could get all four seasons in one day, you could endlessly discuss the forever changing weather. But only superlatives applied to the blue, blue sky here, the unvarying sunshine.

Outside, she saw another lovely morning. So? Every morning was beautiful here. She could not believe it ever rained, or was cold; there could never be grey skies or a chilly wind. This was paradise, and if she and Raphael had not become duellists in a fight she dared not lose they could have been idyllically happy here.

It was the perfect spot for a honeymoon. Her face tightened. She lay back against her pillows, staring at the sky, and then Melina came back to collect her tray, making her jump and hurriedly rearrange her face.

'Guess who just rolled up here in a big estate car to whisk her darling Maestro off on a sightseeing trip around the island.'

Annis stiffened, her face carefully blank. 'Diona Munthe?'

'You win first prize!'

Annis looked out of the window again. The radiance seemed to have gone out of the morning. She forced herself to shrug and say, 'Well, it's a lovely day to go sightseeing. I'm sure he'll enjoy himself. Is there much of the island to see?'

'He will probably have a whirlwind tour and end up at the villa where she is staying. A cosy little party for two.' Melina gave a defiant toss of her head. 'Don't look at me that way! She wants him alone, so that she can flatter and cajole him. I think she wants him to write music for her—songs, an opera, who knows?'

'Yes, I've picked that much up,' agreed Annis flatly.

'Well, there you are, then! I've lived with her, I know the way she works. She is this sort of woman. While she was ill in bed, she was on the telephone all day. To men. Calling all over the world. The bill Mr Diandros will be getting!'

'Perhaps he will ask her to pay the phone bill.'

'No, he will pay—but he can afford it. Mr Diandros is short and fat, and can be very bad-tempered. But he is very rich. You think he lent her this villa because he likes her singing?'

Annis refused to speculate on Diona's relationship with the Greek tycoon, although she had rapidly realised what it must be! Melina gave her a cynical smile, answering her own question. 'No, I don't think so.'

'I'll get up and dress now,' Annis said, hoping that they would have left before she got downstairs. She didn't feel like watching Raphael being carried off by that singing piranha fish.

'Well, I'll go and give Raphael a hand getting ready. That's one thing Diona won't be eager to do! It isn't easy to feel romantic about a man half covered in plaster! What about you?'

Annis turned pink. 'Me? I don't know what you're talking about. There's no romance between me and Raphael.'

Melina gave her a smile. 'I meant, did you want any help getting dressed?' she blandly asked.

'Oh.' Annis bit her inner lip. She had thought Melina was asking something very different, and she still thought so, especially seeing a mischievous, teasing light in the other girl's dark eyes.

Annis said coolly, 'I can dress myself now, thanks.'

Melina took the tray to the door, then turned to say, 'I have an idea! If you don't need me, and Raphael is out, I shall be at a loose end for the morning. Why don't I take you for a drive? You haven't seen much of the island.'

'Great idea,' Annis said at once, her eyes bright and rebellious. Why should she let it bother her what Raphael was doing? It was a superb day, a pity to waste it indoors. She would like to see the rest of the island; her only brief glimpse of it, the day they first arrived and drove to the villa, had been enough to make her eager to see it all.

She dressed slowly and went downstairs, expecting to see that Diona and Raphael had left, but found Diona alone, drinking black coffee on the terrace. She looked round at Annis, her magnificent eyes hostile.

'Still here?' she sneered.

'Obviously,' Annis said shortly, turning to go again.

Diona's brows curved upward distastefully. 'It won't do you any good, you know, clinging on here. You have no claim on Raphael; he didn't cause that earthquake, and, if you're hoping that by hanging around you can make him interested in you, you're wasting your time!'

'Don't judge me by yourself!' muttered Annis, and saw Diona flush darkly, her features tight with rage.

'You flatter yourself! Obviously, you have no idea who I am! Raphael and I are both musicians, artists, our work is all important to both of us, and we're going to be working closely together in the future. We understand each other in a way you couldn't even begin to comprehend! I don't need to clutch at excuses to get close to him; I'm not some starry-eyed fan impressed by his fame and his money. I have plenty of both myself. My interest in Raphael is very different from yours!'

Was it? thought Annis, staring at her. Diona might claim she was interested in working with him, but Annis had seen her looking at him in a much more personal way.

At that moment Raphael came slowly out of the house, leaning on his two crutches. He halted, picking up on the atmosphere between them, and Diona sprang to her feet and walked over to him, her body sinuous as a snake in her tight-fitting dress. She slid a hand under his arm, smiling up at him.

'The car's right outside, I'll help you into it, darling.'

'Thanks,' he said, leaning on her slightly as they came towards Annis. Raphael paused to consider her, one brow slanting upward. 'Are you coming on this tour of the island?'

'No,' she said, beating Diona to it. 'Melina's taking me out.'

'Come along, darling, we don't want to miss the cool of the morning,' Diona said smoothly. 'After noon it will be too hot to drive around.'

Raphael nodded to Annis. 'See you later, then.'

She watched the car move away, a knot of despondency inside her. Diona made her feel so inadequate. The woman was right, of course. She and Raphael had everything in common. What did Annis have in common with him? Nothing.

Melina hurried out. 'Sorry I've kept you waiting; I had to change.' She was out of uniform and wearing brief pink shorts and a low-cut black top; her tanned legs were bare and she wore thin-strapped pink sandals.

'You look stunning!' Annis said, smiling at her.

'Thank you!' Melina said, looking pleased. 'So do you.'

Annis had put on a green and white cotton sun-dress; casual beach wear was out of the question for her with her leg still in plaster, and she envied Melina for being able to wear shorts and a brief top.

'Would you mind if we happened to run into someone?' Melina asked offhandedly as they went out to the car.

Annis gave her a quizzical grin. 'Who might we happen to run into?'

'Oh, a guy I know,' Melina said, wide-eyed and innocent, and Annis laughed. 'Oh, he would not come with us,' added Melina. 'But I thought we might stop for lunch somewhere, and...but if you object, then...'

'Don't be silly, Melina. I'd like to meet him. What's his name?'

'Yanni. His family keep a little taverna down the coast.'

'Ah! Where we would stop for lunch, right?'

'Right.' Melina giggled again.

'Where did you meet him?'

'His family and my family were neighbours when I was little. His mother is fond of my mother.'

Annis understood the delicate situation; it was not an arranged marriage so much as one that would make both families very happy.

Melina helped her into the passenger seat of an open-topped, rather beaten-up old sports car. It had a few dents in the side, its paintwork was scratched and rusting, but when Melina climbed behind the wheel and turned on the ignition it started with a roar like a racing car.

'Good heavens!' Annis said in amazement, and Melina grinned triumphantly at her.

'Is a very good car, even though it is old. Yanni's brother Georgi has a little garage, next door to the taverna, and he worked on my car for nothing. He is very kind.'

They drove for an hour along the coast, through fishing villages clustered around tiny quaysides, where a few tourists wandered in shirts and shorts, sat at quayside cafés and drank tiny cups of strong coffee, or explored the dark little shops up narrow, whitewashed alleys. The sun was brilliant, blinding, the wind blowing through the car refreshing on their hot skin.

They stopped for coffee in one seaside village, where they were stared at by little boys and barked at by thin-ribbed dogs. Annis took the opportunity to do a little

shopping there, in a winding street of whitewashed
houses, little shops, cafés and churches, which wandered behind the seafront. By then the sun was rising
higher and she was grateful for the black shade of the
close-set houses. She bought some inexpensive gifts at
tourist shops, and went back to find Melina sitting at
their table in the café, sipping at a glass of iced water.

'Did you get what you needed?' asked Melina. 'Can
we go now? I think we should drive on to Yanni's taverna, if you're ready.'

They got back into the car and turned inland, to drive
on narrow, mountainous roads with dusty and pitted
surfaces. On either side stretched moorland, rough with
heather and gorse, fragrant with clover, the purple
flowers of thyme, the spikes of rosemary, and noisy with
small, golden bees which fumbled their way from flower
to flower to flower in the summer air, seeming drunk on
pollen and dew. There were olive groves stretching up
the hillsides, old whitewashed churches whose black-
robed priests stared out at them from the shadows within,
and houses on stilts, with pine trees shading their
gardens.

'I much prefer it up here in the hills to the tourist
places down by the coast,' Annis said dreamily, staring
out of the car, and Melina nodded, smiling.

'This is very Greek, yes? I love it up here too.'

'It's very different from Manchester!' teased Annis,
and they both giggled.

It was noon when they drew up outside the taverna
towards which Melina had been driving. A dog emerged
from beneath the terrace and barked at them, then recognised Melina and came to greet her, tail wagging, and
while she was making a fuss of him the family came out
of the low, white-painted house, smiling a welcome.
Melina introduced Annis, who shook hands with them

all—the short, dark father, the plump and smiling mother, a sister who spoke a little English, and Yanni himself. Melina was right; he was good-looking, and typically Greek in appearance, with the usual dark hair and eyes, the olive skin and tan.

'Melina is teaching me to speak English,' he told her, shaking hands. 'How are you doing? OK?'

She grinned. 'I'm fine, thank you. How are you?'

'OK,' he said, looking pleased with himself.

His family were staring at Annis fixedly; they said something in Greek, nodding, and Melina nodded back, replied in the same language. Realising that they were talking about her, Annis asked her, 'What did they say about me?'

'Oh, that if they did not know you were English they would be able to tell at once because you could not be anything else!'

'Is that a compliment?' Annis asked wryly.

Melina laughed and spoke to the family in Greek again, and they all laughed, answering.

'They say yes, it is a compliment, because you have the skin of an English rose!' said Melina, and Annis blushed.

Yanni's family exclaimed with great enjoyment over the soft pink colour flowing up her face, which made her even more self-conscious.

Melina seemed amused. It didn't upset her that her boyfriend and his family should admire Annis, because Melina knew that they were very different types; neither of them needed to feel threatened by the other. Annis had a cool, blonde, very English look, her blue-eyed stare colliding with men's eyes like an iceberg hitting the *Titanic*. Melina was striking in another way, as golden-skinned and luscious as a peach, a Greek colouring that was very dramatic. As they had driven around that morning, through the villages, they had attracted a considerable amount of male attention, divided more or less equally between them. English tourists had barely looked at Annis, but had stared at the Greek girl, who had probably seemed to them excitingly foreign, while young Greeks hadn't been able to take their eyes off Annis.

They had lunch out on the terrace, in the shadow of the vines growing across the wooden beams forming the open canopy. Sunlight flickered down through the green vine leaves, making flowing patterns on their faces, on the table and the floor. Up there in the mountains it was cooler than it was down on the coast.

Even so, the air was very warm as the afternoon progressed, and Annis grew flushed with good food, sweet Greek wine and the heat of the sun.

Their lunch began with enormous tomatoes stuffed with rice and peppers, followed by braised lamb with a green salad sprinkled with home-made fetta cheese, and then green figs.

Yanni served the meal to them, and to a party of American tourists who arrived half an hour after them, in a coach from a cruise ship which was stopping off for the day at the island.

'The taverna has a very good reputation on the island,' Melina told Annis proudly. 'Many people drive up here, especially at weekends.'

'I'm not surprised,' Annis said. 'The food was marvellous.' She yawned, her eyes heavy. 'I think I drank too much wine, though.'

Melina gave her a funny little giggle. 'OK, maybe we go back now, and you can sleep it off on your bed!'

She went off into the house to say goodbye to Yanni, and while she was gone the Americans left, climbing aboard their coach with groans of reluctance at the idea of the long drive back to their ship. The taverna was deserted again; the silence of the mountainside returned. Annis was happy enough to wait; she was almost asleep on her chair, in the shade of the vines.

'Are you ready?' Melina asked, suddenly reappearing, and Annis woke up with a start.

'Oh, yes,' she said, stumbling to her feet, looking for her stick. Yanni handed it to her, and insisted on taking her arm to help her back to the little open-topped car.

'Is OK if Yanni comes with us?' Melina asked.

'Tonight, we go dance,' Yanni said.

'My night off,' reminded Melina quickly, and Annis said that of course Yanni could come, why not?

He climbed into the back seat, and they left, waving to his assembled family who stood on their terrace to watch them depart.

They drove back down to the coast rather faster than they had come up, and Annis felt her heart in her mouth several times as the car screamed round corners on those narrow, bending roads, the tyres sending up choking dust around them.

'Don't look so worried. Is quite safe!' Melina assured her, grinning at her apprehensive expression, and Yanni laughed from the back seat, saying something in Greek. Melina turned to shout back at him, her dark eyes gleeful.

Annis got the distinct impression that Melina was showing off for her boyfriend's benefit, and, although Melina seemed to be a very good driver, Annis was very relieved when they came out on to the winding, coastal road.

Half an hour after leaving Yanni's taverna, they were back at the villa. It had been an eventful drive. Melina had almost gone off the edge of the mountain to avoid hitting an old man riding a donkey in the middle of the road, had thumped over a pot-hole so big that Annis had been sure that the back axle would break, had driven through a flock of hens at a speed that sent them flying, emitting squawks of terror, and had at one point almost spun off the road trying to pass a much slower vehicle foolish enough to be in front of them.

All these exploits had been greeted with hoots of laughter from Yanni. Annis had closed her eyes, turning very pale and praying silently.

Melina had seemed completely oblivious of the silence beside her. She had been too busy chattering to Yanni. But as they came within view of the big white villa, she apparently noticed that Annis was very quiet, but put this down to exhaustion, and reproached herself for having allowed her patient to overtire herself.

'I should not have kept you out so long,' she said, eyeing Annis sideways. 'You must go straight to bed; you can have supper in your room.'

Yanni asked, 'What? What?' and Melina answered him in rapid Greek. He made a soft, anxious noise of sympathy, and as she parked in front of the villa he leapt gymnastically out of the car, opened the passenger door and, before Annis realised what he meant to do, scooped her up bodily into his arms and began carrying her up the terrace steps.

Annis was so startled that she instinctively clutched at him, her arms going round his neck. 'I'm too heavy, put me down!'

Yanni didn't understand. He smiled down at her, a flash of even white teeth in his smoothly tanned face.

'OK, gorgeous!' he said in a distinctly American accent, and Annis couldn't help giggling.

Her grin died, though, as someone stood up on the terrace. Raphael's face was harsh, his brows drawn in a frown that made Yanni halt in his tracks, looking nervous.

'Where have you been all this time?' Raphael snarled. 'And who is he?'

'Put me down, please, Yanni,' Annis said quietly, refusing to let herself be terrorised. Yanni carefully lowered her into one of the chairs arranged around the table on the terrace, and Melina hurried up to give Annis her stick, which had been left behind in the car. Annis met Raphael's angry eyes, her chin up, her own gaze cool and level. 'Yanni is a friend of Melina's. We have been having lunch with his family.'

Raphael went on glowering, his mouth set, and that made her angry.

'What do you mean by snapping at me, anyway?' she muttered.

His eyes were dark wells of anger and pain. She froze as she delved into them and suddenly saw that something was very wrong.

'What's happened?' she asked, her mind whirring anxiously. Was it something to do with his hands? Had he hurt himself while she was out? It was serious, that much she knew. Her own nerves shrieked at what she saw in Raphael's darkened eyes.

He took a long breath, then in a ragged voice he said, 'Carmel has collapsed—she's on life support again.'

CHAPTER NINE

THEY flew to Athens that evening in the private jet which had brought them to the island in the first place. Raphael, Annis discovered, had been making a number of arrangements while he waited for her to return to the villa.

He had called the Athens clinic where they had been treated, and the specialist had said that he would fit them both into his schedule at once, so Raphael had rung Mr Diandros and told him they would be leaving the villa immediately. When he'd heard the reason for this sudden change of plan, Mr Diandros had insisted on sending his plane to the island to pick them up, take them to Athens and from there on to London.

'It will save us a day,' Raphael said curtly. 'We should be back tomorrow evening.' He looked at his watch, his frown etching itself deep into his forehead. 'Can you pack and be ready in fifteen minutes? The car should be here by then, to take us to the airport.'

'I'll help her,' Melina said. She looked at Yanni apologetically and said something in Greek. He shrugged, answering, then turned to Annis and held out his hand.

'Goodbye. Nice to have met you.'

She smiled. 'And you, Yanni. It was a wonderful lunch.'

Yanni gave Raphael a polite nod and went out to Melina's car while she and Annis went upstairs.

152

'Luckily I haven't much to pack,' said Annis, opening the suitcase Melina got out of the wardrobe and placed on the bed.

Melina opened drawers and cupboards and brought the few contents over to Annis, who packed them neatly.

'Poor Raphael. He must have been on the phone all afternoon. I wish I'd been here, I could have done that for him.'

'But then he would have had time to think and worry about his sister,' said Melina.

Annis grimaced. 'That's true. I hadn't thought of that. Maybe it was best that I wasn't here. At least he has been too busy to start imagining the worst.'

Melina frowned. 'What is that? I didn't understand . . . what is wrong with his sister?'

'She has a kidney disease. She has been ill for four years, but I thought her treatment had stabilised it and she could lead an almost normal life. Apparently I was wrong.'

'With a serious condition like that, you can never make a real prognosis,' Melina said soberly. 'She has children, didn't you say?'

Annis nodded. 'Two. They are very young—Sylvia is eight and Robert is six. If they lost their mother, it would wreck their lives, poor kids.'

'Oh, don't be gloomy,' said Melina. 'I'm sure her doctors are doing everything they can, and these days they can do far more for kidney patients than they ever used to be able to do.'

Annis nodded, looking round the room. 'That's the lot, I think. If I've forgotten anything it can be sent on.' They closed the suitcase, and Melina looked at her ruefully.

'It has been so sudden! We had such fun today—and suddenly you are leaving. I shall miss you.'

'I'll miss you, too,' Annis said. They had become good friends over the weeks they had spent together. 'Next time you're coming to England, remember, we would love to have you stay with us. My mother would like to meet you. We must keep in touch, Melina. Look, I'll give you my address.' She scribbled it hastily on a pad by the bedside. 'You will write to me, won't you?'

Melina nodded. 'I don't write good letters, but I will write.'

'Will Mr Diandros give you a week off, do you think?'

Melina made a face. 'I shall be lucky!'

'Well, he's being very kind to us—sending his private plane back here to get us. He must be a nice man.'

'Oh, he loves to mix with artists and musicians, famous people like Raphael,' Melina said with a cynical expression. 'He's not so kind to people who work for him.'

'Well, I hope he lets you have time off to spend with Yanni, and if you two do marry I hope you'll send me an invitation.'

'OK, sure,' said Melina, blushing. Raphael shouted from the bottom of the stairs that the car had arrived. Melina picked up the case and carried it down for Annis.

They said a final goodbye on the terrace. Annis had been concealing something in a capacious, brightly coloured beach bag which she had bought only that morning. Before she and Raphael climbed into the back of the waiting car she produced a little parcel, gift-wrapped in silver foil.

'This is just to say thanks for everything, Melina. You're a wonderful nurse, and I'll write and tell Mr Diandros so when I'm back in England.'

Melina was astonished, not having expected a present, and took it with wide eyes, beginning to stammer.

'No speeches,' Raphael said brusquely, holding out his own hand, which held a small white envelope.

'Goodbye, Melina, and thank you. I'm very grateful for the way you've put up with me. Please buy yourself something pretty with the cheque. You deserve it. As Annis said, you are a wonderful nurse.'

He didn't wait for her to answer; he swung himself down the steps to the car and Annis limped after him. Melina hugged her, and Raphael said impatiently from the car, 'Come on, Annis! We haven't got time for any lengthy farewells.'

'Brute!' Annis muttered, and Melina laughed, then helped her into the car. A moment later the car was moving and Annis waved from the back seat until the other girl, standing on the terrace of the white villa, was out of sight.

'Clever of you to have a present to hand,' said Raphael, leaning back with a faint sigh into the corner of the car. 'A cheque is a bit of a cop-out, but I didn't have time to get her anything. What was in the parcel?'

'A red silk blouse I managed to buy while we were out this morning. She was admiring them, so I knew she would like it. She left me by myself, so that I could buy a present for my mother, and I bought a blouse for her at the same time. It was lucky I did or I wouldn't have had a present to give her. I must have had a sort of premonition that I'd need it sooner than I thought.'

'I wish you could have one now and tell me if Carmel is going to be OK,' he said bleakly, and she put a hand on his arm to comfort him.

'She will be, Raphael! She has these crises from time to time, you know that.'

'This one is different,' he said, and then his mouth tightened and he turned his head away and fell silent.

What did he mean by that? she wondered anxiously. What was different about this crisis? Was it more serious? She watched him sideways from under lowered

lids, wishing she dared slip her hand into his, put an arm
around him, but she didn't quite have the courage.

They spent the night in the Grand Bretagna Hotel, in
rooms which were side by side. Annis lay awake for some
time listening to the muffled sound of Raphael moving
around his own room. He was not making much noise—
indeed, she got the impression he was trying to be very
quiet—but it was obvious that he could not sleep and
was walking restlessly round and round like an animal
in a cage. Raphael was terrified of what he might find
out tomorrow. He had lived for weeks with the possibility that he might never be able to play the piano again,
at the same level. Tomorrow he would know for certain,
and he was on edge.

Annis wanted to tap on their connecting door, go in
to him, comfort him, but she couldn't do that.

Next morning they drove to the clinic to see the
specialist who had been in charge of their treatment while
they were there after the earthquake.

They saw him separately. Annis saw him first,
underwent a lengthy examination, and was eventually
pronounced quite fit again. Her ribs had been un-
strapped by Melina days ago, and now the plaster cast
was cut off her leg by a nurse while she gritted her teeth,
expecting it to hurt. There was some discomfort when
the plaster was removed because the hair on her legs had
stuck to it, but it was only momentary.

She was escorted by the nurse to the hospital canteen
to have a cup of coffee while she waited for Raphael,
whose examination would take longer.

Annis sat at a table near the door, drinking cup after
cup of strong Greek coffee, watching for Raphael with
her nerves leaping. The time ticked slowly by without a
sign of him, and then she saw him walking towards her
in the old way, lean and graceful as a panther, that tall
body held upright, without his sticks. The plaster casts

were off his legs, but she had expected that. There had never been any real fear that Raphael might not walk again.

Her eyes flashed up from his legs to his hands, her heart in her mouth as she looked to see if they were still bandaged. They weren't. She saw their skin, strangely pale after having been bandaged for so long, hidden from the sun. Raphael was automatically flexing the long, slim fingers and she took a hard breath, then focused on his face, trying to guess from his expression whether the specialist had given him bad or good news.

He halted, looking into her eyes, and suddenly smiled with such blinding radiance that she knew the news was the very best. She stumbled to her feet, tears gleaming on the ends of her mascara-darkened lashes, met him halfway across the room and flung her arms round him, too happy to care about anything but Raphael for that instant.

'It's OK, isn't it? Your hands...they're going to be OK!' she said huskily, clinging to his shoulders.

Raphael bent and kissed her fiercely on the mouth, then lifted his head and looked down into her upturned face with that brilliant, relieved smile.

'It's more than OK,' he said. 'It's bloody marvellous. I can play, my darling. I did. They have a piano in the staff rest-room, and the old boy took me along to see if I could play, and I could. Oh, I'm a little rusty—I haven't touched the keys for several months now—but I had no difficulty getting my span, and as I loosened up I could feel it there. A few weeks' solid practice and I'll have it all back.'

She realised that all around them people were staring openly, and stepped back, flushed and still smiling tremulously. 'I'm very happy for you, Raphael. It's wonderful,' she said. 'And what about your other injuries? Did he say you were quite fit? What about your legs? Your ribs?'

'I've been given a clean bill of health, but I still have to attend physiotherapy for some time, apparently.'

'Same here,' she nodded. 'He said I was in perfect shape.'

Raphael's grey eyes mocked, running slowly down over her figure. 'I agree with him.'

Her heart beat fast. 'Shall we go?' she said hastily, turning towards the door, and Raphael fell into step beside her.

A taxi had brought them from the hotel that morning and they took a taxi back into the centre of Athens. The streets were as crowded as ever; an endless traffic jam stretching through to Syntagma Square meant that they spent ages getting back to their hotel.

'Did the doctor say it was OK for you to fly back to London tonight?' Annis asked, her eyes fixed almost with incredulity at the shimmering white columns of the Parthenon which stood up against the blue Athenian sky above the road. She could never get used to seeing it so casually; it was always a sort of mirage to her.

'No problems there at all,' said Raphael, and Annis smiled, nodding.

'Nor for me. So we'll be on our way home tonight. I can't wait to walk through that airport and——' She broke off with a cry of shock and alarm.

'Oh... I'd forgotten... I haven't got a passport!'

'Oh, yes, you have,' Raphael said casually. 'Didn't I tell you? I must have forgotten. When the workmen dug out the hotel office, they found the hotel safe. Apparently it was lined with lead, so none of the contents were burnt during the fire. They found a pile of guests' passports in it—including yours.'

Annis took a relieved breath. 'Oh. That's marvellous. Do you know, I'd forgotten that we had had to hand over our passports to the hotel receptionist when we arrived. How do I claim my passport, then?'

'It was sent to Mr Diandros and he sent it on to me,' Raphael said coolly.

She stared sharply, her blue eyes narrowing. 'What? How long ago?'

He shrugged. 'Oh, a week or so.'

'And you didn't tell me?' Dark red flowed up her face; she was so angry she wanted to hit him.

'I must have forgotten to,' he explained, and she was almost speechless. Almost. Not quite.

'Forgotten? You forgot to tell me? How could you forget something as important as that? You deliberately didn't tell me!'

'Why should I do that?' he said smoothly, then bent and whispered in her ear, 'The taxi driver is staring, Annis.'

'I don't care if he is!' she muttered, glowering.

Raphael suddenly leaned forward, tapped the driver on the shoulder and said something in Greek. The taxi stopped and Raphael opened the door, got out, and held out a hand to Annis, who automatically got out too, rather bewildered when she saw that they were not in Syntagma Square yet. Raphael paid the driver, and the taxi slowly moved on in the traffic jam.

'What are we doing here? Where's our hotel?' Annis asked.

'It's nearly noon, and I don't know about you but I'm starving. I know a great restaurant a few streets from here, where you can eat fresh seafood, pick out your own lobster from a tank and choose how you have it cooked.'

'It would stick in my throat!' she muttered furiously, and ran across the road, bolting through the slowly moving traffic while cars hooted and their drivers screamed in rage at her. Annis ignored them, heading

for the shade and privacy of the National Park, with its
enormous palm trees and wide, gravelled walks. Raphael
caught up with her a moment later, rather out of breath
because of the unaccustomed exercise.

'Annis, wait...' he said breathlessly, and she looked
at him with ice-blue eyes.

'Go away, Raphael. I don't want to eat with you; I
don't really know if I ever want to see you again. I'm
very angry with you—you tricked me into staying on
that island by letting me think I didn't have a passport.
You knew my passport had been found ages ago, didn't
you?'

'I needed you with me,' he said huskily, reaching for
her.

She knocked his hand off her arm, turning on him
angrily. 'Is that why you spent so much time with that
singer?'

He caught her shoulders and drew her under the shade
of one of the towering palms, looking down at her, his
breathing audible and uneven. 'Jealous, Annis?'

Her face flamed. 'No, I'm not! Jealous about you?
Don't make me laugh. But I won't have you lie to me—
you didn't need me, you just wanted to force me to stay
there so you could torment me whenever you felt like
it...' She stopped, confused, not sure what she was
saying, and Raphael's grey eyes glittered.

'How could I torment you if you hate me, Annis?' he
whispered raggedly.

She bit her lip, angry with herself for having made
such a slip-up. She had to pull herself together. Now
more than ever it was essential that she get away from
Raphael and never see him again.

'Leave me alone, Raphael,' she said in a low, dull
voice, pulling herself free. 'Let me have my passport
when we get back to the hotel, will you?'

He stopped looking amused, his face harsh. 'I see! You've turned against me again, have you? When I joined you in the hospital just now, you kissed me with tears in your eyes, as if you really cared whether I could play again or not, as if what happened to me mattered as much to you—but suddenly I'm Public Enemy Number One again and you hate me. Why, Annis? Just tell me why! You change moods too fast for me to keep up with you. I never know what you're going to say or do next, and I'm a man who has enough instability in his working life. I don't want upheavals day and night in my home too. You're too moody and unpredictable for me. So, OK, when we get back to London we say goodbye for good.'

He turned on his heel and walked away, and Annis followed slowly at a distance. They walked around the square to their hotel and each went to their room without speaking. Annis sat on her bed, tears slowly falling down her white face. He hated her. And who could blame him? The ache inside her wrenched her apart, but she was powerless to do anything about it. She could only endure this final separation, as she had the other.

She heard footsteps outside her door, recognised them at once, and froze, a hand at her trembling mouth.

Raphael knocked briskly twice. She slid off the bed, ran her hand over her wet eyes, took a couple of deep breaths, then went to the door.

He didn't even look at her, just handed her a brown envelope, and then was gone. She closed the door again, and tore open the envelope, unsurprised to find her passport inside. Now she could back to England whenever she chose. She did not have to go with Raphael in the Diandros private jet. Wasn't that what Raphael had just told her by his icy silence?

She lay down on her bed and tried to sleep, but the noise of Athens outside the hotel kept her wide awake.

She was very hot, too, so she took a shower and changed into another dress, decided she was hungry after all, and went downstairs to the hotel dining-room to eat a light lunch.

Afterwards she decided to go for a walk. She needed to keep moving because her brain was so restless. She could not decide what to do. Her head said one thing, her heart another, and Annis swung helplessly between the two of them.

On her way across the hotel lobby she caught sight of Raphael sitting on a leather couch, his face drawn and pale, his eyes fixed on the floor.

She hesitated fatally, and he looked up, as if becoming aware of her presence.

His eyes were bleak and Annis could not walk by. She went over to him and sat down next to him, her hand instinctively reaching for his. For a moment she thought he would resist the touch, then his fingers curled around hers tightly and he hung on as if for dear life.

'Have you heard any more news?' Annis asked gently, and he sighed, nodding.

'The hospital are as cagey as ever, but the ward sister did admit that her condition was giving rise to some concern.' His teeth snapped together violently. 'Why do they have to be so damn pompous? Giving rise to some concern! Why can't they use plain English and say she's seriously ill? Do they think I can't take the truth? Anyone would think I were a child instead of a grown man.'

With her free hand, she stroked the hand she held, soothing him automatically, as if he were, indeed, the child he claimed he was not.

'They are taught to wrap things up so as not to alarm relatives unnecessarily. After all, people often recover completely after they've sailed pretty close to death, and the authorities don't want either the patients, or their relatives, thinking gloomy thoughts, so they——'

'Lie,' Raphael said, his mouth twisting cynically.

'Wrap things up!' she corrected. 'Don't let yourself think that Carmel may die, Raphael. When you see her, you don't want her picking up negative thoughts, do you?'

He shook his head. 'Of course not. I can lie too.' He looked down at their linked hands. 'Are you coming back with me tonight, Annis?'

She knew she should say no, she wasn't, but she also knew she couldn't let him fly back alone. Raphael's love for his sister had always been one of the most important things in his life. It was a toss-up whether Carmel, or music, mattered most to him. Annis had never believed that she could compete with either his career or his sister, she knew she ran them a poor third—and she also knew that if Raphael lost Carmel he might well go to pieces. She could not let him go back alone to face his sister's possible death.

'Yes,' she said quietly, and Raphael sighed, then lifted the hand entwined with his, turned it palm upward and placed a long kiss in the warm centre of her palm. She trembled, her breath catching, and he looked up at her, his eyes dark with emotion.

'Thank you. I don't think I could face it alone. Will you stay in Manchester until . . . until I know——?' He broke off, his mouth unsteady, then said roughly, 'For sure, one way or the other?'

'If you want me to,' she agreed slowly, trying to think. 'I . . . I'll stay in a hotel near the hospital, if you like.'

'No, in the house,' he said, frowning. 'I'd like to bring the children back . . .'

'Back?' she questioned, puzzled.

'They're staying with my cousin in Birmingham; she was the only relative who could take them. I want to bring them home—would you look after them for me for a few days, Annis?'

She bit her lip, appalled by the thought of being in that house again, yet unable to explain why, and

Raphael's face tightened. Brusquely, he said, 'I know it's a lot to ask. Forget it.'

'No, no,' Annis said hurriedly, hating herself. 'Of course I'll look after them, I'd love to, I was only hesitating because . . . well, I've never looked after children, and I'm not sure I'd be any good at it.'

'You were always wonderful with them,' Raphael said, his face lightening again.

'I've babysat for an hour or two, but never been alone with them, in complete charge . . .' She didn't know how she could face going back to the Manchester house. She had had too many nightmares about it. But Raphael's anxious frown had gone and she could not bring it back, so she forced a smile and said flatly, 'But if it will make you feel any easier, of course I'll do my best.'

'Thank you,' he said on a sigh. 'You've no idea what a relief it is to know they'll be with you. I suppose I could get a professional in to look after them, but I don't want to leave them with a stranger who doesn't care about them. They need to be with people they know and trust. Oh, they could stay on with my cousin, she's kind-hearted and well-meaning, but she lives a long way from Manchester, and they should be near their mother, just in case . . .' He stopped, his face rigid, then went on flatly, 'She might want to see them if she recovers consciousness. And anyway, I think they should be in their own home. They must be scared and bewildered, poor kids, not knowing what's going on—no mother and their father gone——'

'Gone?' Annis interrupted, startled, her blue eyes very wide and incredulous. 'What do you mean? Where has Barry gone to?'

Raphael stared back, his mouth a tight, white line. Annis felt her stomach clench in a spasm of fear. Why wasn't he answering her?

CHAPTER TEN

RAPHAEL frowned harshly. 'Didn't I tell you? I must have said something...'

Annis shook her head, her face pale, stiff with shock and nerves.

Raphael grimaced. 'I thought I did—when I told you Carmel had collapsed. I said something then, surely?'

'You didn't mention——' She broke off, swallowed, still hating to say that name. It conjured him up, and she preferred him safely locked away, like a genie in a bottle. Huskily she tried again. 'You didn't say anything about...Barry. Has something happened to him? An accident?'

'No accident,' Raphael said shortly, the lines of his face hard, charged with rage. 'That's what caused——' He broke off as a voice floated to them across the crowded hotel lobby, a woman's voice, high pitched and indifferent as to whether it was heard or not, or perhaps the pitch of it had been deliberately designed to catch his ear.

'Hey, look! Isn't that Whatsit? You know, the conductor...what's his name? Spanish name—I'm sure it *is* him! He and his orchestra have been touring around Europe, everywhere we went he had been there first. Let's get his autograph. He's rather dishy, don't you think, Jenny, if you like the Mediterranean type? And I do!'

Annis shot a glance past Raphael and saw a full-breasted, skinny-hipped girl in a scarlet shirt and tight trousers, avidly staring.

Raphael did not look round; he merely glowered. 'Damn. Obviously we can't talk here. There are too many people around. Someone is bound to overhear us.' He got up and pulled Annis up with him, steered her towards the lift, ignoring the hurrying footsteps following them. 'Don't look round!' he ordered in a very low voice. The lift doors closed on them a second later and the lift began to rise.

'The trouble with being in the public eye,' Raphael said grimly, 'is that fans think they own you, and journalists think you're fair game. I may be, but my sister doesn't deserve to be pilloried because of me. I don't want Carmel or the children reading about themselves on front pages.'

They had reached their floor. Raphael urged her towards his room, unlocked his door and ushered her into the luxurious one-bedroom suite which his Greek tycoon friend had booked for him. Annis stood looking around in surprise; she had not realised that Raphael had a small sitting-room as well as a bedroom, and her blue eyes held faint amusement for an instant. Well, of course Raphael was given star treatment! What had she expected?

'Sit down, Annis, you're very pale,' he said impatiently. He gestured to a velvet-covered couch by the window looking out over Syntagma Square, and, moving like a sleep-walker, she obediently went over to it and sat down. Raphael didn't join her, he walked up and down the room with a caged ferocity, his body tense, his hands in his trouser pockets, his black head bent as he talked.

'I got the news all at once, on the phone, from my cousin yesterday. It was like being punched in the stomach.' He halted at the window, not looking at her, just staring out at the blue Athenian sky, then abruptly went on, 'Three days ago, Barry ran off with the nanny who had been looking after the kids.'

Annis gave a stifled cry and he looked down at her. 'That was what made Carmel——' he broke off, his tanned throat moving as he swallowed.

'Made Carmel collapse?' Annis finished for him, her blue eyes enormous in her pale face.

'Yes,' Raphael said harshly. 'He and the girl sneaked out of the house while the kids were at school. There was a cleaner in the house. They told her they were just going shopping and Carmel was asleep, not to disturb her until the doctor arrived—he was coming to do a routine blood test. The cleaner let him in, and then left, but the doctor noticed a letter on the table in the hall, saw it was addressed to Carmel, and took it up to her. She opened it, read it, and...' His eyes flashed. 'If the doctor hadn't been there when she collapsed, she might have died! They knew the risk of that. When I think what might have happened! The kids would have had to find their own way way home from school when their nanny didn't arrive to pick them up, and they would have found that letter, given it to their mother, and can you imagine the traumatic shock for them when she...'

Annis caught his hands and held them tightly. 'Don't, Raphael!'

He sat down beside her, a heavy sigh wrenched from him. 'It makes my blood boil, Annis. How could he do this to her? Oh, I know it hasn't been easy for him the last few years while Carmel has been so ill, but I've done what I can to make their lives bearable. He hasn't had to find money for rent and I paid for the nanny, damn her—and the cleaners. I could afford it and I knew Barry couldn't, it was no problem to me, and I thought he loved my sister. I can't say I ever had much time for him—he isn't on my wavelength, we're from different worlds, and Barry isn't exactly a very admirable character. He spends money like water, he's always in debt, he's selfish, weak and spineless, but I did believe he loved Carmel. It never entered my head that he would ever walk out on her and the children.'

'It entered mine,' Annis said harshly, and Raphael looked at her in blank surprise.

'Did it? You never said anything to me about not trusting Barry!'

She took a long, deep breath. 'How could I?' she whispered. 'I knew how much Carmel loved him; I knew it would shatter her if she ever found out Barry could look at another woman.'

Raphael stiffened, his expression changing, staring fixedly into her wide, nervous blue eyes. 'What made you think he might?' he said slowly, and she could see that he had caught on to her tone and was beginning to guess now, his mind leaping ahead.

She had held it back so long, been so careful never to give him or anyone else any hint, that it was the most enormous relief to say it aloud at last.

'He was always making passes at me.'

Her voice shook, rough with an anger she had turned inwards on herself for years, as though it were her fault, as though she might have made it happen somehow, even though she knew that wasn't true. She had hated even to be in a room alone with Barry; she had not wanted him to come anywhere near her. Yet at times she had wondered...had any of it been her fault? Had there been some way she could make a joke of it? Get him to stop?

Would Raphael blame her? Men often blamed the woman, took it for granted that a woman had to have invited it, provoked it, even if only by the way she dressed, by smiling, being friendly...just by breathing!

She sat very still, watching Raphael watching her. He was as white as paper, his facial bones locked in a rage so powerful that she got the impression he dared not speak or move for a moment. He sat rigidly beside her, hardly breathing. Was he angry with her—or his brother-in-law?

He parted his teeth and bit out, 'Go on. There's more, isn't there?'

Well, he had himself under control, which made it easier, but she began tentatively. Once she had started, though, the words poured out of her like molten lava which had finally burst up to daylight from the hidden dark.

'It was always when you were away on one of your tours. You used to say to me, "Go and see Carmel whenever you can, won't you?" and I couldn't tell you why I didn't want to go, could I? I couldn't tell Carmel, either. She used to ring me and say come to dinner, come to lunch, come and have tea with the children, and I would have to go, because I was trapped. I ran out of excuses sooner or later, and so I would go and try never to be alone with Barry, but he would insist on driving me home, and if I said I'd rather take a taxi or walk he would say to Carmel, "You talk sense to her, darling"...' She shivered. 'It was so horrible. And I simply did not know what to do. I felt like someone trying to walk on eggshells—one false move and I could smash all those lives: ours, Carmel's, the children's... And Barry was well aware of that. He made sure I understood what would happen if I said anything. He had spelt it out for me the first time he tried to get me into bed——'

'Into bed!' Raphael broke out hoarsely, trembling with anger.

She nodded, her face as pale as his, her blue eyes full of a mixture of shame and bitterness. 'Yes, of course! You don't think he just wanted me to give him a kiss? Oh, he was serious, he knew what he wanted and he made sure I did. I told him, "No!" over and over again,

I kept out of his way if I did have to go to the house,
but he always managed to get me on my own sooner or
later, and it always ended the same way, in a horrible,
silent fight because I couldn't scream or make a noise
or Carmel would have heard, and Barry knew I dared
not make a sound. He took every advantage of it. You
say he's weak? I wouldn't call him that. I'd say he was
utterly unscrupulous; he was downright merciless to me.'

Raphael ground his teeth audibly. 'I wish to heaven
you'd told me! I wouldn't have told Carmel, I'd have
dealt with it without bringing her into it! I'd have beaten
him to a pulp!'

Annis laughed without amusement. 'Yes, that was
what I thought you might do. That's why I couldn't tell
you.'

'To protect that little weasel?' he asked, eyes flashing,
and she shook her head.

'No, of course not. To protect Carmel. I said I'd have
to tell you if he didn't leave me alone, and he laughed
at me. He had it all worked out, and he told me what
would happen if I said anything. You would go crazy
and beat him up, he said, and then how could we all live
under the same roof? He and Carmel would have to go,
would have to live in some small, cheap rented flat—
and that would kill Carmel.'

'The scheming, twisted little blackmailer!' Raphael's
hands screwed up into fists; a dark red colour was
crawling up his face. He watched her with eyes which
held a sort of horror. 'Annis,' he whispered,
'you...he...didn't...?'

'No!' she cried out, shuddering. 'Oh, no, never—I
couldn't have borne it, to let him touch me. He made
me sick. That was why I had to go away.'

'Aah...' Raphael let out a long, rough sound of com-
prehension, his face in confusion, breaking up, suddenly seeing everything. 'That was it!'

She nodded wearily. 'Yes, that was why I walked out of your life.'

Raphael leapt to his feet with an almost animal spring, his long body so tensely held that he had to unleash it. Annis sat and watched as he paced from one end of the room to the other. He wasn't looking at her; he was staring at nothing, his features set like stone, only his grey eyes alive, and there was such violence in them that she was frightened of him, of whatever he was thinking.

He stopped suddenly, in front of her, stared down at her, his dilated pupils like glittering jet.

'You dumped me rather than tell me what that bastard was doing to you?'

The harsh voice made her nerves leap. 'I'm sorry,' she whispered.

'Sorry? Sorry?' he exploded and she talked hurriedly, trying to calm him down, pacify him with words.

'Try to understand how I felt. What was I to do? I was trapped. It was like being buried under that hotel— I couldn't see my way out, I was alone and in the dark and terrified. Surely you can imagine how it was? I tried to find some way out, but every way was blocked.'

'You could have told me!'

'How could I if it meant Carmel's finding out? I couldn't tell you anything, for Carmel's sake, and the very idea of giving in to him was...' she shivered, her mouth writhing in distaste '...nauseating. So what could I do? If I had stayed and married you, I would never have had a moment's peace in that house. Every time you went away—and you are away half the year or more—Barry would have pestered the life out of me. Believe me, I racked my brains for an answer. I thought of going on tour with you, but you kept saying you didn't want that. You knew I liked working in the Manchester office, and you wanted me to have my own life, my own job, not to become an appendage of yours...'

He groaned, putting his face in his hands. 'I thought that was what you wanted! To be independent!'

'It was, and I knew that if I threw up my job and went on tour with you people would think I was going to keep an eye on you, being possessive and smothering!' She made a wry little face at him. 'None of the orchestra takes his wife with him!'

He shook his head. 'All the same, in the circumstances——'

'No, that wouldn't have worked, Raphael! So I wondered if I could tell you I wanted another house, a place of my own somewhere else, but how could I do that? It's your family home, you love it and I knew you wouldn't want to leave it. You and Carmel would just have thought that I didn't want to share your house with her. Carmel would have been hurt, and that was the last thing I wanted to do—hurt Carmel. I'm very fond of her.'

'She's very fond of you,' Raphael said quietly.

She smiled. 'Still? I expect she stopped liking me when I walked out on you. Carmel was always as loyal to you as you are to her.'

'She's sees things other people never notice,' he said, face thoughtful. 'Funnily enough, she had been worried about you for ages before you left. She told me she had thought you might be ill, that you had seemed very edgy and disturbed for months.' He laughed shortly. 'Thank God she never knew why!'

'Yes!' Annis said, lifting her eyes to him, and nodding. 'And she must never know!'

Raphael looked sharply at her. 'But now Barry's gone...'

'That's different!' she said earnestly. 'Think about it, Raphael! She can hate that girl for stealing him, blame her, not Barry, find excuses for him—but if you tell her about me, she would be forced to realise it wasn't the first time, that it wasn't necessarily the girl to blame, that Barry hadn't been faithful until that girl tempted him. Oh, you could assure her it wasn't my fault, and she might accept that, she might not blame me for what happened, but would she still feel the same about me? I could never be her friend once she knew. There would be that between us for the rest of our lives, because she loves Barry, and she's unhappy enough without giving her more bad news. So, promise me you won't tell her!'

He slowly nodded. 'Very well, you could be right. I'm no expert on female psychology. I can't fathom the way women's minds operate. I couldn't even work you out, could I?'

'You didn't know——' she began and he interrupted harshly.

'No, I didn't know what was going on! You didn't trust me enough to tell me!' He stared down at her, a muscle working beside his pale mouth, tension in every line of his body. Annis was frightened by that look. She crouched there, in a corner of the couch, her arms wrapped around her body, like a small animal trying to look smaller, trying to disappear. He was looking at her as if he hated her, breathing thickly, darkness in his grey eyes, and it made her want to cry.

'When you ran out on me, telling me you were going away with some other man, it turned my world upside-down!' he grated. 'Do you have any conception what you put me through? I almost went out of my mind, trying to find out where you were, who the guy was! If I'd found you both, I'd have killed him with my bare hands.'

He flexed them, those large, powerful hands which had such delicacy when he played, and yet such strength, and Annis stared at them with fixed attention. She almost believed him capable of murder at that moment, and shivered.

'I couldn't work,' he muttered. 'Couldn't even sleep, couldn't think of anything else!'

She looked unhappily at him, her mouth quivering. 'Raphael, I only went because I couldn't see any other way out. I'm sorry——'

'Don't say that again!' he snarled. 'I might just hit you!'

She shrank back on the couch. His rage scared the life out of her. Raphael had always been temperamental, given to inexplicable swings of mood, but she had got used to that. She had seen him angry, she had seen him light-hearted or euphoric, but this savagery was something new.

He stared down at her, brows very black in his pale face, and she wished she knew exactly what he was thinking—or would it be better not to know? 'Was there another man?' he asked abruptly, making her jump.

It threw her into confusion; she could only stammer. 'I . . . I . . .'

He snarled again, bending towards her menacingly. 'And this time I want the truth!'

She swallowed, and didn't try to speak that time. She just shook her head.

He exhaled sharply and walked away across the room. Annis watched him nervously, her mouth dry with panic as he turned and came back towards her.

'Has there been anyone else since you left me?' he demanded, and her lashes fluttered down against her flushed cheeks.

She shook her head again, and Raphael made a low, rough sound, reached down, grabbed her shoulders and pulled her to her feet. 'Look at me!'

She kept her lashes down, watching him through them, but afraid to let him see her eyes, and after a minute he caught her chin in one hand and tipped back her head so that she had to look up at him. Her wide, shy blue eyes lifted then, to meet his probing stare; she didn't try to hide anything, because she couldn't, not any more. She had lied and pretended for too long. She allowed him to read the emotion in her gaze, and Raphael drew another thick, audible breath, then his mouth came down in relentless possession and her lips softly surrendered without a struggle.

Her arms went round his neck and she swayed against him in a blind delirium, forgetting everything for that instant except the heated insistence of her own desire.

The need had been dammed up inside her for too long. It crashed out then, and swept away all inhibitions, all pretences. She kissed him hungrily, touching his hair, his face, his neck, feeling the warmth and roughness of the male flesh under her passionate fingertips, and she heard Raphael groaning under her mouth, heard the heartbeat deep inside his body quickening, thudding, felt the wild pulse in his throat as her fingers brushed against it.

'Darling, oh, darling,' she whispered under his kiss, and his mouth lifted then. He looked down into her blue eyes, his face darkly flushed, his breathing erratic.

'Tell me,' he said hoarsely. 'Tell me you love me, you never stopped!'

'I love you. I never stopped loving you,' she murmured, lifting her mouth eagerly for his kiss, and Raphael's mouth swooped down to take her lips again. His hands began to slide softly down her body, teasing and tantalising her with light caresses while she trembled, moaning, her own hands busy exploring him, the long, slim back, the wide shoulders, the narrow hips.

Raphael suddenly picked her up bodily, without taking his mouth from hers. Annis instinctively clung, like ivy winding itself around a great tree, her slender body utterly abandoned to him, her arms round his neck. She didn't need to ask where he was going; her head swam with the realisation, and she was hardly able to breathe, a wild eroticism beating through her veins.

He laid her on the bed in the further room, breaking off their kiss, and knelt beside her, watching her with eyes that leapt with fierce excitement. She gazed back, her body a coiled spring waiting for him to set it free. His hand moved, deftly undid the three white buttons on her dress, while she watched, flushed and dry-mouthed, her tongue tip moistening her parched lips. His fingers slid inside the dress, an intimate voyage of discovery that made her shake violently, reaching out for him.

He pushed her hands down, shaking his head, his grey eyes glittering. 'Slowly, darling. Slowly.' His hand cupped her breast and she moaned, closing her eyes. He stroked the nipple lightly and it hardened with sharp arousal. Raphael bent his dark head and his tongue tip teased, making her gasp, shaking from head to foot, her head turning from side to side on the pillow in restless desire. He slid a hand under her back and lifted her, slid the dress off her shoulders and downwards, threw it to the floor and pulled her slip straps down, his head burrowing between her breasts. She stroked his cheek, her eyes still closed, passion burning deep inside her.

'Forgive me, Raphael,' she whispered, her fingertips winnowing his hair. 'I can't bear it if you're still angry with me.' She couldn't let him make love to her with that violence inside him.

He knelt up, staring down at her. 'Forgive you?' he said roughly. 'For leaving me without a word? That isn't so easy. I went through hell for you, Annis, but I can forgive you even for that. What I can't forgive you for is not telling me what Barry was up to! He put us both through all that grief, when he could have been stopped if you'd only trusted me enough to tell me what was going on! I would have moved heaven and earth to protect you, you should have known that.'

'I knew that!' she said unhappily. 'But...oh, I explained...'

'I know, I know, my darling,' he said huskily, putting a finger on her lips. 'It was an impossible situation for you. Don't you think I can see that? If you loved me——'

'How can you say that?' she burst out shakily, tears in her eyes. 'Can't you see I love you so much it nearly killed me to leave you?'

'Don't cry, darling,' he muttered, kissing her wet lids. 'You make me hate myself. You misunderstood what I was trying to say. It's me who should be begging for forgiveness, not you. I believe you loved me. Yet you went away, for Carmel's sake. You loved me, but for the sake of my sister you left me. How can I be angry with you for that? How can I be selfish enough to try to put myself first and my sister second, when you could do the opposite? You hurt me badly and I wish you could have felt able to confide in me but I blame myself, not you. I'm ashamed you couldn't trust me enough to tell me what was happening.'

'It wasn't that I didn't trust you!' she denied, and he shook his head at her.

'No, it was just my damn temper, wasn't it? You were adult enough to understand what had to be done. But I wasn't adult enough for you to turn to me.'

She looked ruefully at him. He was too extreme, too intense to be able to keep himself on a tight rein where his emotions were concerned; that was why she had not told him. That was what she loved in him, too.

'It had nothing to do with being adult,' she said with a gentle little smile. 'It's just the way you are, Raphael— in your music and in your life. All or nothing, that's you. And I wouldn't want you any other way. I love you, darling.' She touched his cheek with tender fingers, smiling at him. 'Let's forget Barry, and just think about ourselves.'

He caught her fingers and kissed them softly, his eyes passionate. 'We've got hours before that plane goes,' he said, and Annis smiled.

'Hours,' she agreed huskily.

Raphael began to unbutton his shirt.

They arrived back in Manchester in pouring rain, the empty streets like running rivers as they were driven straight to the hospital where Carmel was on a kidney machine. She wasn't conscious, the ward sister in the intensive-care unit told them, but they could go in to see her.

'How serious is it this time?' Raphael asked, his voice deep and rough with fear, and the woman smiled at him with professional calm.

'She's ill, Mr Leon, but she has been this ill before and come through it. I can't give you a definite answer yet. You can talk to her specialist tomorrow; he may have more idea by then.'

Annis took Raphael's hand and felt his fingers close tightly around hers. 'Let's go and see her,' she said, and he nodded.

Carmel was a waxy, yellowish colour, her face puffy, her closed lids thick, mouth swollen and colourless. Raphael stood looking down at his sister bleakly, still holding on to Annis.

'Thank God you're with me. I don't think I could bear this on my own,' he muttered.

'You don't need to, I'll always be here,' Annis said, squeezing his fingers, and, as if the sound of her voice had penetrated to wherever Carmel's tired brain had retreated, the sick girl's lids rose and her eyes focused dazedly on Annis's face. Carmel looked puzzled, frowned faintly, then looked at Raphael. This time recognition flickered into her face, and she looked as if she was trying to smile.

'Hello, dear,' Raphael said huskily, bending closer. 'Look who I've got with me!'

Annis bent too, smiling. 'Hello, Carmel.'

Carmel's eyes moved back to her, stared, her lips moved soundlessly. Raphael seemed to understand what she wanted to say without its needing to be said. He nodded to her, and smiled.

'Yes, we're back together again. This time for good. Being buried together in that hotel in Greece made us realise we were meant for each other!' he joked, then his grey eyes grew serious. He lifted their linked hands so that his sister could see them. 'We're getting married as soon as you're well enough to be at the wedding, dear, so hurry up and get back home, because I'm in a hurry to put my ring on her finger.'

Carmel's mouth curved painfully into that sweet smile Annis remembered so well. This time Annis, too, could lip-read what she tried to say. Very glad.

'We're bringing the children home,' Raphael told her. 'Annis will move into the house to look after them. You needn't worry over them; they'll be fine with her.'

Carmel looked at Annis. Thanks, she mouthed.

'I'll enjoy it. Your kids are great,' Annis said, and Carmel's eyes smiled, then she gave a weary little sigh and her lids fell.

They had to leave a few minutes later, chased out by the ward sister, but they were back next day, early, before leaving to pick up Carmel's children. The ward sister stopped them in the corridor and told them that they couldn't see Carmel; the specialist was with her. They would have to wait.

'I'd like a word with him, anyway,' Raphael said, and they sat down in the corridor outside Carmel's room until the door opened and the specialist emerged with a little troop of students following him. Raphael got to his feet at once. The specialist gave him a quick, sharp look, then offered his hand.

'Raphael Leon! This is an unexpected pleasure. I have a number of your recordings, and I'm a great admirer of your music.'

Raphael inclined his head, impatience only shown by a flash of his grey eyes. 'Thank you. You're very kind.' A polite pause, then he said, 'You've been visiting my sister—how is she this morning? Are you satisfied with her condition?'

The specialist drew in his lower lip, his head to one side. 'Satisfied? No. But I am not unhappy. She shows definite signs of improvement since yesterday. If she goes on improving at this rate, we can start feeling optimistic, I think. She is still a very sick woman, but she is no longer on the dangerously ill list.' He looked at his watch. 'Well, I have the rest of my round to do. Nice to have met you, Mr Leon. If I bring in a couple of records, will you autograph them for me?'

'Very happy to,' said Raphael, and then the great man and his acolytes moved on to another patient, leaving Annis and Raphael sitting in the starkly painted corridor, listening to the ebb and flow of the hospital.

'You may have to wait half an hour,' the ward sister warned.

'We'll wait,' Raphael said.

The sister shrugged and went about her business, and Raphael gave a long sigh of relief and weariness. Annis slipped her hand into his and he gave her a sideways smile of love as he enfolded her fingers in his own, their shoulders touching. They did not speak; they did not need to. They just sat together, holding hands, waiting with patience, and perfectly happy.

*   *   *

Six months later, Annis, in dusty jeans and a white sweater, was on her knees in front of a large packing-box, unwrapping the contents while from a chair Carmel tried to guess what they would find. 'A giant toaster? A fondue set modelled on the Albert Hall? A life-size statue of Diona Munthe?'

'Ssh…' Annis laughed, removing the last layer of tissue paper and staring down into the carton. 'Oh!'

'What? What?' Carmel asked, getting up to come and see for herself what Annis had found. 'It is a statue!'

'Not of Diona, though.'

'Thank heavens!' Carmel teasingly added, and Annis smiled absently, gently disentangling the statue and lifting it out.

They both gazed at it, and Annis sighed. 'It's lovely, isn't it? What would you say it is? Art nouveau?'

'Later than that. More art deco,' said Carmel thoughtfully.

'Yes, I think you're right. It's definitely post-First World War, from the late twenties, isn't it? It would look terrific in Raphael's music-room.' Annis hunted through the wrappings. 'Who sent it, though?' She found the card a moment later and read it. 'Gunther? Oh, he's that German conductor Raphael gets on with so well, isn't he?'

'That statue looks as if it might be German,' said Carmel, running a hand over the smooth planes of dark stone. 'Or East European, anyway. I really like it.'

Annis watched her, glad to see the relaxed posture, the colour in her face. Carmel's skin had a pink glow again; she had more energy; that terrible sadness had left her eyes; she was beginning to move out of the shadows, Annis thought. Now and then she still looked lost and sad, but those times came less and less, thank heavens. Barry had left a void in her life, of course. She had relied on him throughout her married life, but now that he had gone Carmel was beginning to rely on herself. She had realised that her children needed her now more than ever. They missed their dad, too. They had been just as hurt and bewildered by his desertion, and for their sake Carmel had put a brave face on her own sorrow. At first her smiles had all been pretence, but lately Annis felt Carmel was smiling spontaneously, genuinely.

Raphael had made every effort to stay close to home over the past months, so that he was always there if Carmel needed him, and Annis was happy for him to put his sister first for the moment. They had decided to put off their marriage until Carmel was much better. They were together a great deal, anyway, since Annis was living with Carmel and her children, helping them all to adjust to a new way of life without Barry. As time went by, though, they both became impatient, frustrated, wanting to be alone more, to have their own home, begin their life together, yet at the same time not wanting to wreck Carmel's new-found stability.

It was Carmel herself who had resolved the problem. Raphael was booked to do a two-month-long concert tour of South America beginning at the start of March, which his manager said it was too late to cancel. He and Annis had been unhappily discussing the long absence this would mean when Carmel had surprised them by asking point-blank why they didn't use the trip as a honeymoon. They had stared back at her in stunned silence.

'Otherwise, you're going to be apart for months. You don't want that, either of you—do you?'

'No,' Raphael had said, taking Annis by the hand and holding it tightly.

Annis had looked anxiously at his sister. 'But, what about you, Carmel? We can't both go away...'

'Don't worry about me, I'll be fine. I've decided to go back to work.'

That had shaken both of them, and Raphael had looked startled and worried. 'What do you mean, work?'

'I've got a job in an architect's office, as a receptionist. It's just for three days a week, and it's nice, light work. All I have to do is sit there, smile, answer a phone and talk to people.'

'Carmel, if you need money, I'll gladly help,' Raphael had begun, and his sister had shaken her head at him.

'It isn't just money. I want a job. I'm not an invalid, you know. I just have to be careful, take my medication, not overdo things. I'm bored with staying at home. I'm looking forward to starting there. They seem very nice people in the office, and the boss is a charming man, going a bit bald but with a lovely smile. So you won't need to worry about me, Rafe.'

'What about the children?' Annis had asked uncertainly.

'They're at school all day, and I'm going to get someone in at weekends to help out, if I need it. I can manage!' Carmel had looked determined, her jaw stubborn. 'I've got to get my life in order, I won't go on relying on other people any more. I think I let myself give in while B...' She had paused, biting her lip, then said bravely, 'While Barry was around to be relied on. Maybe I made his life impossible—have you ever thought of that? What sort of life did he have here? I wasn't a real wife to him any more; I wasn't a real mother. I'm not a total invalid, but you all cosseted me and spoilt me until I acted like one. Well, from now on things are going to be different. I want to run my own life, look after my own children, make my own decisions. Before it's too late, I'm pulling myself together, and don't try to stop me, Raphael.'

He had looked into her eyes, given her a wry, admiring smile. 'I wouldn't dare!'

She had laughed, flushed. 'Good. Now—let's make a list.'

'List?' they had echoed together in blank bewilderment.

'Of what needs to be done. First, what sort of wedding do you want? Big? Quiet? Impressive? Select?' She had grinned at her brother. 'No, don't you answer, Rafe. The bride decides what sort of wedding it's going to be. Annis?'

'Quiet,' Annis said dreamily. 'A church, a white wedding, just family and a few friends. An organ and——'

'A bridesmaid! Me!' Sylvia had exclaimed, coming in from school just then. She had just had her ninth birthday, but was oddly adult for her age, perhaps because of her mother's long illness.

Everyone had laughed. 'And a page-boy?' Carmel had suggested, looking at six-year-old Robert, who had made aghast noises and run behind a chair from which shelter he'd yelled out,

'*No!* Won't be a page-boy. Won't.'

'Scrub the page-boy,' Raphael had said with sympathy. 'When I was Robby's age, I'd have hated the idea too. I'm happy with the rest of it, though. A quiet wedding will suit me.'

They might have known then that their plans would be blown sky-high once the Press had got hold of the news.

As soon as the gossip columns had printed the date of the wedding, they had begun to get phone calls and letters from friends and fans of Raphael, asking to be invited. At first it had been a trickle, then it had become a flood, until now the house was awash with wedding presents and the reception party was going to be enormous. Annis had very few guests on her list, compared with the one Raphael had finally drawn up.

Looking uncertainly at her, he had asked, 'Do you mind, darling? It does seem to have got out of hand, doesn't it?'

'It isn't your fault you're famous,' she had teased, then kissed him. 'It's only one day, then we'll have the rest of our lives together.' Yet at the same time she had wondered how much of him she would actually have, with all these others competing for his attention.

He came into the room while she and Carmel were admiring the statue sent from Germany. 'Who sent this?' he asked, instinctively doing as his sister had done, running a hand along the cool stone.

'Gunther,' said Carmel, going out of the room. 'I'll put the kettle on for some tea, shall I?'

Once Annis would have jumped up, saying, 'I'll do that, Carmel.' But she had learnt to let Carmel do things, so she and Raphael smiled and she said, 'Thanks, that would be terrific!'

Raphael read the card Gunther had enclosed with his present. 'I must write at once to thank him. He won't be at the wedding, of course. He's off to New York tomorrow for Diona's opening night next Thursday.'

'You should be there, Raphael!' Annis said at once. 'It's your music, and you and Diona have worked so hard to get it right. You must be dying to know how it's received. If we weren't getting married, you could have flown there on your way to Rio. You could have conducted! I'm sure you would rather have conducted than have Gunther do it.'

It was an old argument, and he put an arm round her. 'Don't start that again! I'll read the reviews, thanks. I've told you—I'm glad it will be Gunther putting up with Diona's first-night nerves, not me! It's been bad enough for me over the last month, having to cope with her in rehearsal. You have no idea what she can be like...complaints, clamouring for compliments... vicious tempers. That woman is an emotional terrorist!'

'Poor Gunther,' said Annis, meaning it. She was never jealous of Diona now; she had learnt she didn't need to be—Raphael might admire the singer professionally, but he found her exhausting and irritating as a woman. After a few hours' rehearsing with Diona he had come home to Annis drained and at the end of his tether, badly in need of her calming presence, the peace of an evening spent alone with her, listening to his favourite music or quietly playing the piano to her.

Raphael grinned. 'Yes, poor old Gunther! Still, Diona's an amazing singer and we're all ready to put up with a lot from her just to work with her.' He sat down in an armchair and drew Annis down on to his lap, burying his face in her throat. 'Oh, my love, you don't know how much I look forward to getting home to you after a few hours with that tigress of a woman. She eats my energy and spits me out in bits, and then I come running home to you to be put together again...'

Annis softly stroked his thick, dark hair, murmuring wordlessly, as if he were a child. Raphael sighed deeply, his eyes closing.

'I can't wait to be alone with you for two weeks after the wedding!' he said huskily. 'We both need a long holiday, don't we? It has been a hectic six months, for all of us, but you need a break even more than I do. You've been wonderful with Carmel and the kids. You must be very tired, darling.'

'I've enjoyed it, though,' she said, almost surprised by that herself. 'It's been fun, even if it was tiring at times.'

'You like being needed,' Raphael said with tender amusement, staring into her dark blue eyes. 'And you are... I need you more than I can ever explain, my love.'

'Just two more days,' Annis thought aloud, hardly able to believe it was true. Just two more days and she and Raphael would be man and wife.

'Two more days and you'll belong to me,' he said deeply, kissing her upturned mouth.

'We'll belong to each other,' she said, kissing him passionately, her body trembling because she had needed to belong to Raphael for years, and had been frustrated, left empty. She was afraid to risk believing that at last it was going to happen.

She only began to believe it when she was actually on her way down the aisle towards him, with the organ pealing triumphantly, and spring sunlight glowing through the dusty stained-glass windows of the great Victorian church in Manchester, just around the corner from Raphael's family home.

It was not the quiet wedding Annis had dreamed about—inside the church sat row upon row of guests: a few relatives from each side, her mother and some aunts and cousins, some of her friends, and a host of people from the music world who had come to see Raphael Leon get married. Outside the church Raphael's fans crowded. When Annis got out of the bridal limousine she had been taken aback to hear the sea-like roar of them all, to see the strange faces, looking at her as though they might rend her limb from limb for having stolen their god.

She was being given away by her uncle, who had to lean on her, rather than the other way around. Her mother had insisted that she ask him to take her down the aisle, and Uncle John had surprised them both by accepting. He was very frail, needed a stick to walk with, but was quite pink with excitement.

Loveday and Carl had been invited. Loveday, indeed, was Annis's chief bridesmaid. She had been thrilled when Annis rang to invite her. She had been expecting the wedding, but not to be asked to be a bridesmaid. They had kept in touch while Annis was living in Manchester, and she had written a discreetly worded explanation to Loveday and Carl, having guessed that sooner or later the story would break in the newspapers.

Loveday looked fabulous in her long satin dress. The warm apricot shade they had chosen together perfectly suited Loveday's red hair, and gave her usually pale skin a warm glow. There were two small bridesmaids: one Sylvia, Carmel's daughter, the other a seven-year-old who was Annis's second cousin. The little girls wore identical dresses to Loveday and carried Victorian posies, as she did. They all had their hair dressed with fresh flowers echoed in their round posies, and Annis wore real flowers in her hair, too, inserted into the pearl head-dress pinning her long veil into place.

Raphael's black hair gleamed in the dusty sunshine. He looked taller than Annis remembered in the morning suit he wore. Annis felt a qualm of uncertainty as she stared at his long, lean back.

He looked strange, unfamiliar; she felt a sob well up inside her chest and faltered in her next step, almost tripping over her sweeping hem. Her uncle looked down nervously at her. Annis bit her lip, fighting with tears, looked sideways and saw Carmel's affectionate eyes watching her. Carmel smiled a reassurance, understanding the brief panic surging through her, and then Raphael turned, looking for her.

She saw his pupils dilate in startled pleasure at the first sight of her. He had not, of course, seen the full-skirted Victorian-style wedding dress before. There were yards and yards of material in the skirt and the three stiff petticoats beneath it. The bodice had a sweetheart neckline, with a little spray of pink roses pinned there, and down to the waist it was ruched, with pearls stitched here and there. Lace flowed down the skirt, caught up at places with palest pink roses and satin bows. Annis had chosen an ultra-romantic style because she knew Raphael would love the faintly baroque nature of the dress, and because it suited her smooth blonde hair, slender figure and small waist.

She had had her doubts, of course, had wondered if he would like it, and it was a relief to see his face and know he did.

He smiled, mouthing silently, You look beautiful! and she smiled back at him, her eyes dark with love, and took the final step to join him at the altar. Her uncle stood back, Raphael's hand searched for hers, and took it in a possessive grip.

At last their life together could begin.